THE STORM WE FACE

THE DARKNESS WE CRAVE BOOK 3

KATIE MAY

EXPRESSO PUBLISHING, LLC

Cover Design by Melody Simmons

Edited by Meghan Leigh Daigle with Bookish Dreams Editing

CONTENTS

Prologue   1
Chapter 1   3
Chapter 2   15
Chapter 3   27
Chapter 4   34
Chapter 5   40
Chapter 6   46
Chapter 7   54
Chapter 8   61
Chapter 9   72
Chapter 10   80
Chapter 11   91
Chapter 12   100
Chapter 13   108
Chapter 14   113
Chapter 15   122
Chapter 16   130
Chapter 17   138
Chapter 18   148
Chapter 19   159
Chapter 20   168
Chapter 21   176
Chapter 22   184
Chapter 23   193
Chapter 24   200
Chapter 25   210
Epilogue   214

Acknowledgments   217
About the Author   219
Also by Katie May   221

PROLOGUE

ADDIE

I stared at the place I'd last seen him. I stared at the place where he'd made his final stand, where he'd gone out in a blaze of glory. He had always wanted to die like that—a hero.

I let out a scream of anguish, but the sound was lost in the cries. One cry couldn't be distinguished from the thousands of others.

All I could do was stare. I'd loved him, and he was lost to me. Love, I began to realize, was dangerous. It only brought unbearable pain, a pain that could not be put into words.

I wondered, as I stared at a splatter of blood darkening the carpeting, if my love had inevitably led to his death.

CHAPTER 1

ADDIE

*H*e was going to kill me. Of that, I was sure. He was going to kill me and enjoy it, like the twisted psychopath he was.

I leveled a kick at his stomach, but he easily sidestepped it. It felt almost like a dance. Each one of us performed a separate part, a separate move, utterly in sync with one another. Okay, so he was in sync with me. I was floundering in too deep water, trying my hardest to keep my head above. Unlike him, I *didn't* know the moves to this dance. I tried, I failed, but I tried again, ever persistent.

He grabbed my arm, twisting it behind my back, and I let out a grunt of pain. He really was going to kill me. Before I could scream, he flipped me over his shoulder. My back thumped painfully against the grass, and I stared up into my attacker's brown and gold eyes.

"I am going to kill you in your sleep. No, better than that,

I'm going to cut off your balls, feed them to you, then kill you in your sleep," I said from my spot sprawled on the ground.

The bastard in question merely stood over me with an amused tilt to his lips.

I was only going to refer to him as Bastard. I'd made up my mind about that yesterday, when we first began. He didn't deserve a first name.

Or a sexy nickname.

Not that he was sexy or anything. Well, I mean, he was, but…

Bastard's smile had grown, hinting that I might have spoken aloud.

Oops.

"Sarge!" Ronan, bless his soul, called from the doorway. "We need you for a sec."

Bastard, aka Sarge—or Fallon, but it was whatever— offered me a hand. Over his broad shoulders, I could just make out the dusting of sunlight slowly disappearing behind the boughs of trees.

"Get your dumbass hand away from me," I hissed. "I'm content to just stay here."

He raised an eyebrow at me.

"Let me die in peace, please," I added. He smirked but obediently jogged towards the back porch where Ronan was waiting impatiently.

The bastard decided I needed to "train." Apparently, getting kidnapped by one of my boyfriends' psycho ex-girlfriend made it clear how weak and frail I actually was. Thus, Bastard decided to put me on a strict diet and even stricter training regimen.

I'd argued profusely when he first suggested it. I had to get to Atlanta ASAP to see my little brother, Nikolai. I haven't heard from him since the world went to hell, and worry constantly niggled me.

But we weren't able to leave. The boys insisted that we had to collect more supplies since most of ours were lost in an earthquake and Ryder needed time to heal. I hadn't argued after that, especially when I considered Ryder's empty gaze.

Yes, he most definitely needed time to heal.

I myself hadn't fared any better from the kidnapping. My face would always hold a reminder of what that bitch did to us. The scar sliced down my cheek, starting just below my eye and ending near the top of my lip. I didn't know how I felt about it.

I'd always paid tribute to my various scars. They were a reminder of all I had conquered and all that I wanted to conquer. This one was no different, yet I could see Ryder's haunted expression whenever he stared at the line disfiguring my face.

Blame. Guilt. Shame. Something akin to embarrassment.

I understood the expressions he wore all too well. I tried telling him what Liz did wasn't his fault, but he always pushed the subject away with a stupid joke or a sarcastic remark.

He was like me in that way—using wit to hide his pain.

A large figure stood above me, effectively cutting out the sunlight once again. His silhouette would've been almost ominous if I didn't know who he was.

Only one person was that big

"Is this what death feels like?" I asked dramatically, flinging my arms out on either side of me for emphasis.

Calax snorted.

"Don't be so dramatic and get your ass up."

Yup. No sympathy from my giant. If it was Asher or Tamson, they would offer me a massage or a hot blanket. But Calax?

Apparently, I had to suffer through it. Ugh. He was lucky I loved him.

His dark hair was extremely tousled just then. He always had a tendency to run his hand through his hair when he was anxious or upset. Planning our day-long, if not longer, trip to Atlanta would most definitely put anyone in a sour mood.

"Carry me?" I asked weakly, holding my arms up to him. He chuckled but obediently scooped me into his arms as if I weighed nothing more than a baby. Smiling, I nuzzled his neck.

"I knew there was a reason I kept you around."

He turned his face towards mine, and his lips lightly brushed my own. They were as soft as a moth's wing. Tingles of electricity ran through my body at the contact.

"Is that the only reason?" he asked. I enjoyed this side of Calax—the light, relaxed side that remained hidden from the rest of the world. I loved his grumpiness and his protectiveness, but I adored his teasing. It reminded me of when we first met, when I decided I hated and loved him. He was still my mortal enemy, but I figured it wouldn't hurt if we kissed...and confessed our love to one another. Yup. No problem with that.

Bastard.

Smug, sexy, infuriating—

"You're talking aloud again," the smug, sexy, infuriating Bastard pointed out. In reply, I stuck my tongue out at him. His eyes turned heated.

"I can think of better things you could use that tongue for."

Before I could reply—or jump him like I was a dog in heat —the sliding glass door that led to the backyard opened, and Ryder stepped out.

His dark hair had been freshly washed, no doubt from the nearby stream, and he wore a pair of jeans and a white shirt.

The shirt itself greatly contrasted with his dark skin and showcased the many tattoos circling down his large biceps.

He was sex on a stick.

And mine. Did I mention that already?

Not trying to brag or anything...

"Don't hog our girl," he said to Calax lightly, and my heart fluttered at the words. Our girl. Swoon.

I would never get over the fact that these two perfect men decided I was worthy enough to be in a relationship with. To share, some may say, though I didn't like that connotation. It would imply that I'd split my heart and body between the two men. I loved them both equally, as if I had two entirely separate hearts beating inside of my chest. One for each.

Ryder brought out the playful side in me.

Calax was my rock.

And for some miraculous reason, they decided I was deserving of their love and affection. Of course, that meant I had to actually be a girlfriend to these two men. I thought that meant I had to feed them or something? Maybe take them out for a walk? It was a learning curve.

Ryder, seemingly unperturbed that I was in Calax's arms, kissed my cheek tenderly. I glanced under my fringe of lashes, assessing Calax's reaction, but he appeared unbothered by his brother's affection towards me.

Despite declaring his love for me, Ryder had yet to actually kiss me. You know, like *kiss me* kiss me. He gave me a chaste brush of the lips when we were in hell—okay, Lizzy's house, though they were basically the same thing—but never a toe-curling, tongue-humping make out. I was honestly afraid that he didn't want to or something. The boy had kissed a lot of girls, yet he somehow hadn't been able to kiss me?

Puh-lease.

I tried to ignore these insecurities. Ryder was mine in

heart, soul, and body, and I was his. I knew that he loved me, yet the child in me recollected all of those times I'd felt vulnerable and unloved.

Used.

Discarded.

Ryder's hand was still resting on my cheek when we heard the door behind us open. He immediately pulled away from me as if he'd been burnt.

I blanched, though not for the obvious reasons. I wasn't hurt or upset that Ryder hid his affections towards me. We'd agreed to keep our unconventional relationship a secret from the rest of the team.

A team that I may or may not have feelings for.

Yup. I was a nutcase. Apparently, my demented mind decided that two perfect guys weren't enough. Oh no. I had to develop feelings for the other five members of their team as well.

I wasn't in love with them, at least not with all of them, but it was something undefinable that caused my heart to clench painfully whenever they were near. It was lust, yes, but something so much more than that. They each brought out a different side of me, a better side of me, that I had thought didn't exist. They made me want to be better.

My breath left me in an exhale when I saw only Tommy standing on the porch, his eyes narrowed suspiciously.

Tommy was my child. Not literally—I was only eighteen, and he was thirteen—but at least mentally. I didn't think he would appreciate that sentiment though.

"What are you assholes doing?" he asked, cocking his hip to the side and glaring at us through his large glasses. I was pretty sure that he didn't actually need glasses, but had found them inside one of Elena's drawers. His sass was just another reason I loved him. And his penchant for pink, sparkly eyewear. "Not you, Addie. You're not an asshole." He took a

step towards us in what he probably thought was a threatening manner. I'm afraid that it was impossible for him to
look dangerous standing at five feet with his face bloated
from baby fat.

He was honestly kind of adorable.

Raising his eyebrow, he gave me a long look.

"You okay, Addie?" he asked me, voice considerably more
gentle. He leveled a glare at Ryder and Calax, both of whom
towered over his tiny frame. "If I discover that you two are
taking advantage of her, so help me god, I will—"

I cut him off before he could end his threat.

"I'm fine, Tommy. Promise."

If I thought of Tommy as my surrogate son, he thought of
me as his daughter. It was an odd relationship, but it seemed
to work.

After one more glare aimed at the guys, he stomped
towards the door, calling over his shoulder, "Sarge called a
meeting."

"That kid is getting on my last nerve," Ryder muttered. I
merely planted a sloppy kiss onto his cheek.

"You're just jealous."

He snorted but didn't contradict me.

Still in Calax's arms, we walked into the living room of
Elena's house. The couches were now moved to form a small
semi-circle. Tamson and Asher were sitting on the couch,
both wearing small smiles. Tam, my timid friend, met my
gaze, blushed, and then immediately glanced down at his
feet. I hated that I made him feel self-conscious, but I also
didn't know how to stop it.

Talk to him?

I doubted he would be receptive to that. Asher offered me
one of his brilliant smiles, his shaggy blond hair brushing his
eyes. It was in desperate need of a cut, but I secretly loved his
disheveled look.

Ronan was on the loveseat, his legs kicked over the arms. His green hair was stylishly spiked and his unicorn tattoo peeked over the edge of his shirt. I still wondered about the purpose for that particular tattoo, but there had never been an appropriate time to ask.

Declan was leaning against the doorframe, muscles straining against his black T-shirt. I had a complicated relationship with Declan. Complicated because I used to love the shit out of him, but now I barely knew him. I hoped that we could rekindle the friendship we once had. Years had gone by with me believing he was dead and him believing I hated him. It was hard for anyone to get past that.

I waved my hands to garner his attention.

"You're doing a mighty good job of holding up that wall," I signed. *"Whatever would we do without your help keeping the house from falling?"*

His lips pulled into a tiny smirk, but that smirk instantly disappeared on his face when he took in the position I was in. Namely, still wrapped in Calax's arms.

I knew that he, as well as the rest of the team, was aware I was dating Calax. I was also aware that they didn't necessarily agree with that decision, though I couldn't discern if their disdain came from annoyance or something else entirely.

I wondered what they would do if they discovered I was dating Ryder as well.

Knowing Ronan, at least, he would want to join.

Not that I would object…

Pinching Calax's arm, I indicated for him to drop me on my feet. At first, I thought he wasn't going to listen as his arms tightened around me, like an impenetrable fortress between me and the outside world. His arms were a heavenly place where I didn't have to worry about pain. Heaving a heavy, if not resigned sigh, he set me down.

"Where is the bastard anyway?" I asked. Said Bastard was noticeably absent from the meeting he'd apparently called.

Such a bastard.

"Really, Adelaide?" a cold voice asked, accompanied by a raised eyebrow. I folded my arms over my chest and glared at him as he walked through the archway. His hair was pulled back into a knot on the nape of his neck, a few strands escaping and curling around his ears.

"I'm pissed at you," I retorted oh so wisely. To emphasize my point, I rubbed at my sore shoulder. He merely rolled his eyes at my dramatics before turning towards the rest of the group.

His team.

Fallon refused to sit, though that was no surprise. He always had to be the tallest, most imposing figure in the room. With his broad shoulders and penetrating eyes, he most definitely succeeded.

"Excuse me!" I said, before he could speak. I waved my hand in the air. Fallon pinched the bridge of his nose and closed his eyes.

"You don't need to raise your fucking hand, sweetheart," he muttered. "We all know you're just going to talk anyway."

I frowned.

He may be right, but still. Dick.

His smile grew, hinting that I may have spoken that insult aloud. Again.

"I have a few topics I would like to bring to the committee's attention today," I said seriously. Ronan coughed to cover up his laugh. "The first one is concerning Atlanta. I don't believe that everyone should go with me. I vote that I travel by myself."

I should have really considered a career in politics. I was a damn good diplomat.

Before anyone could protest, I held up a hand. "Calax can

come with me, for obvious reasons. And Ryder can come to...sing me to sleep. Not any other reason." I knew that it would be wishful thinking on my part to believe that they'd let me go alone. Damn them. At least I nailed the whole subtlety thing concerning Ryder. The assholes would never suspect we were dating. Singing a person to sleep was a completely valid reason for coming with them on a dangerous journey across the country. Right?

"And Ronan will probably want to go because his brother is going, so I guess he can come too." I paused, considering my words thoughtfully. "Fallon is probably going to want to go, but I doubt Fallon would leave the rest of them behind. Declan, of course, is welcome to come. Tamson can come too, since his ninja skills would come in handy. If they all come, I'm going to need Asher to calm myself down. Heaven forbid that I'm stuck with all of these assholes without Asher. So yeah. Only those people can go."

I blinked innocently, glancing from one face to the next. Fallon raised a dark eyebrow at me.

"Kitten," Ryder said softly. "You literally just invited everyone."

"No, I didn't!" I protested, but my mind immediately replayed my monologue.

Damnit. That was a fail.

Fallon, still looking too damn amused, clapped his hands together.

"Now that Adelaide has given us all permission to join her, shall we move on?"

"I didn't mean to do that." I crossed my arms over my chest with a huff. Sometimes I wondered if it would be best if I glued my mouth shut. I had a serious case of word vomit.

The whole goal of my spiel was to convince the boys *not* to follow me. Obviously, I hadn't succeeded. I really sucked at the whole people thing, despite my repeated attempts at practice.

"The second thing I would like to address is your team and school. I'm not stupid. I know it's more than a normal boarding school. I want answers, and I want them now. I can't keep living in the dark. I mean, I'm a ride or die type of person, but I want to know where we're going and why we have to die." I leveled each of them with my best glare. The guys exchanged rapid glances with one another before Fallon released a heavy sigh. His thick lips were pursed as he considered me.

"You're right," he admitted at last. "You deserve to know everything."

Calax's hand tightened over mine, and Ryder turned to stare at me pleadingly, begging me to understand what I was going to hear. I had the distinct feeling that these answers, the answers I wanted so desperately they were almost a physical ache, were going to change my life.

"We should probably start at the beginning," Fallon said.

"The beginning?"

"There was a reason we were at the resort to begin with."

"Which was?" I was beginning to become irritated. Fallon had a tendency to give me vague answers. The more he talked, the dizzier I became. Crossing my arms over my chest, I waited for him to collect his thoughts.

"For your parents," he admitted after an excruciatingly long moment of silence. I shifted. Whatever I'd expected him to say, it wasn't that. What did my parents have to do with a boarding school?

My confusion must've been evident on my face, as Fallon released another heavy sigh. His hand crept up to pinch the bridge of his nose.

"I suck at explaining this," he mumbled beneath his

breath, and I resisted the urge to make a very inappropriate joke about sucking.

"Look, Addie," Ronan interrupted, turning to stare at me. He leaned forward so his elbows rested on his knees. "We don't actually go to a normal school. We were chosen because we each displayed a unique set of skills that made us valuable." He ran a hand through his green-tipped hair. It was beginning to grow out, and I could admit to myself that I would be upset to see the green dye leave his dark hair entirely. Granted, he would always be my leprechaun. What could I say? I was a sentimental bitch. "What I'm trying to say is—"

"What he's trying to say is that we work—worked for the government," Tam broke in. "We work for the government, and we came to the resort in order to investigate, and eventually arrest, your parents."

What.

The.

Fuck?

CHAPTER 2

ADDIE

I stood there, staring at the men who'd quickly become my entire world. They gazed back at me, eyes earnest, if not pleading. I tried to process Tam's words, tried to understand the implications of such a simple sentence.

Arrest.

Parents.

Government.

Nothing made sense.

"Kitten," Ryder said. "Say something."

I blinked at him.

"I don't know what to say."

Because my world has just been turned upside down. All of our interactions had been a lie. Had they even wanted to be my friend, or was I just a mission to them? That thought made my heart squeeze painfully as if held together by iron clamps. I remembered my first meeting with Ronan, the first time I rested my eyes on Asher.

I remembered my conversations with Calax. How he'd conveniently moved into an apartment complex my parents owned.

Oh god.

"Addie, I see the wheels in your head turning." Calax almost sounded desperate, an emotion I doubted he was familiar with.

I only managed to croak out one word. "Explain."

It was Fallon who spoke, finally regaining his cool. He straightened his spine and leveled me with a penetrating stare. It felt as if he was seeing through my layers of clothes and into my very soul. I couldn't help but squirm at the scrutiny. My soul was dark and tarnished. I feared that if he looked any closer, he would see how broken I actually was.

"Your parents were believed to be involved with an international drug cartel, among other things. Human trafficking, for one. Murder." He continued to stare at me, eyes assessing. I shifted in my seat, both at his words and his unflinching eyes. "We were investigating a particular case. A Mexican drug lord named Jose Hernadez."

"Papa Jose?" I asked, stunned.

"Huh?" Ronan broke in, eyebrow quirked.

I knew exactly who he was referring to, and I may or may not have known that Papa Jose wasn't a grade A citizen. Don't judge.

"He told me to call him Papa Jose," I filled in helpfully. Tam and Asher exchanged startled glances. "I liked him. He would give me candy when he came to visit."

"Addie..." Calax began in his usual reprimanding tone. "How many times do I have to tell you? Don't take candy from drug lords."

"Bygones be bygones." I waved my hand dismissively.

They were investigating my parents? Papa Jose? Again, that thought didn't unsettle me. It was surprising, yes, but somehow, I'd already suspected as much. I knew that the boys weren't the standard, all-American high schoolers. They were so much more than that.

"So..." I trailed off, unsure of how to phrase my next question. On one hand, I didn't want to offend any of the guys, especially Ryder and Calax. But...you know what they say. Curiosity killed the petty bitch. "Was anything true? Our friendships? Our..." I glanced between Ryder and Calax, too quickly for anyone to notice. "Relationships?"

I saw hurt flash in Calax's normally impassive expression, and I hated myself for putting it there in the first place.

"I didn't know who you were when I first met you," Ronan offered at last. "I knew they had a daughter, but you were not my assignment. Actually, it was Elena's team's job to get close to you. To become your friend."

A snort escaped, unbidden.

"That turned out well."

"No shit." Ronan's lips quirked. "All I knew was that you were a strange, slightly crazy girl that I had to get to know better."

"None of us looked at you like a mission, Kitten," Ryder said softly. He reached forward to squeeze my knee. "Sure, we wanted to protect you and care for you, but that had nothing to do with the case or your parents. That was solely because of you. We wanted to be your friend because of who you were as a person, not because of who your parents were."

My heart swelled at hearing his words. I offered him a brilliant smile, and he immediately met it with one of his own. Calax, however, was *not* smiling. His scowl was firmly directed at the wall above Fallon's head.

Well shit. I sucked at this girlfriend thing.

Food. I needed to offer him food.

Reaching into my pocket, I shoved a granola bar into his large, calloused hand. Tamson had given it to me earlier that day to eat after training. I was happy that I had saved it though. Calax glanced from the bar, to me, and then back to the bar again. Tentatively, he peeled back the paper and nibbled on the edge of the bar.

Finally, *finally*, he offered me a small smile. A breath of relief instantly escaped me.

Best. Girlfriend. Ever.

I turned back to the conversation, aware that I had missed the ending of Fallon's spiel. From the amused glint in his eyes, I figured he was aware of that as well.

Another thought swirled through my head, gaining traction the more I thought about it. I bit my lip, staring at each of their beautiful faces. The question continued to niggle at me, and I finally dared to ask.

"Do you know?" I whispered.

"Know what?" Ryder asked.

"What started the end of the world. Do you know?" My voice was soft. It might've given the impression that I was calm, but I was anything but. My thoughts were running rampant and unsupervised through my mind. I felt betrayed, angry, upset.

I felt it all, and it almost consumed me.

I didn't expect them to answer. If anything, I expected them to deflect.

"Global warming," Fallon said at last. His fingers drummed a pattern against his jean-clad legs. I watched the rhythmic pattern of his fingers, utterly entranced. The golden bands of his rings glistened in the candlelight.

"Global warming?" I repeated stupidly. Wasn't that the answer to everything? Was he joking? Was he trying to be funny?

I couldn't help but snort. Fallon? Funny? Good grief. Hell would freeze over before that day would come.

"That's a theory," Tam continued. His face lit up, as it always did when he discussed something that interested him. I yearned to see that brilliant smile on his face every day. Hell, I yearned to be on the receiving end of such a smile. I mentally scolded myself, breaking out of the wistful fantasies that held me hostage and focusing on his words. "When the ice caps melted, it released a parasite that had been stuck in there... well...forever. It can survive both in water and on land."

I turned over the information Tam had given me. While I'd studied biology, I was never an expert in it. My parents much preferred my curriculum to be math and business based. So this? I had no idea how plausible of an explanation it was. It could've been bullcrap for all I knew.

Ronan continued, "It enters a host—us—and takes over a section of the brain."

"The limbic system," Tam filled in. "The part that makes you want to fight or flight. It helps you understand stimuli and act accordingly. This parasite? It messes with that. The only option you have is to fight. It makes you behave with an uncontrollable rage. A rage that is almost primitive in nature..." Tam trailed off, face contemplative.

"You were told all of this?" I asked, turning from face to face. Asher appeared almost sheepish at my accusation, and Calax's scowl deepened when I turned towards him.

"By some of the top scientists," Fallon said, nodding. "I'm friends with some people high up."

This was almost too surreal. I wasn't supposed to receive the answers like this. I'd thought there would be trial and error before I would be able to come to a conclusion. It felt almost cheesy, in a sense, like a badly scripted scene in a B-rated movie. Everything was a coincidence, I realized. It was one of the numerous facets that pieced together fate. Maybe we were fated to come together. I was the mission, and they were the team. I had the questions, and they had the answers. Fate had a mind of its own, and it made you its bitch more often than not and squished you like a bug beneath stiletto heels. Still, my stomach churned almost violently as I leafed through all of the information given.

I felt betrayed. I was running down this race blind, and I'd dumbly assumed they were doing the same. It struck me deep to realize I'd been alone this entire time. They hadn't trusted me with their secrets, yet they'd expected me to offer up my own. And I had, like the desperate, scared girl I was.

I knew I should be grateful that they were finally telling me the truth, yet the sly voice in my mind wondered if they still would've told me if I hadn't asked. The voice said no.

Not Calax. Not Ryder.

Not Ducky.

"I need a second," I muttered, standing and walking towards my designated bedroom.

"Addie," Ryder called after me, and I flinched at the use of my name coming from his mouth. I wasn't Kitten at that moment. Just Addie.

And I hated her.

"I need a damn second," I snapped. Before he could respond, I threw myself inside my bedroom, my back to the door.

Fuck them.

Their secrets. Their lies. Their avoidance of the truth. I was beyond furious. They had betrayed me, and the scars cut deep.

"You look pissed," a voice said, and my head snapped up. Elena stood in the room, absently grabbing duffle bags off of the top shelf in the closet. Her blonde hair was braided back from her stupidly pretty face, and she wore a baggy T-shirt and ripped jeans.

"I am pissed," I said before I could stop myself. It was very easy to overlook the fact that Elena hated me with a passion. Sometimes, she almost seemed to be…nice. I knew that she was jealous of my relationship with the guys. She loved them, and it pained her that they never felt the same way. Her hostility towards me was somewhat understandable, if not completely uncalled for. You couldn't pick and choose who you loved. It just happened, a natural part of human nature.

"They told you?" she guessed, and I bristled. It may have seemed petty, but I didn't like the imperiousness in her tone, as if she thought she knew them and the reasoning behind their actions better than I did.

"Yeah," I said, deciding to play civil. "They told me. I just don't understand *how*. How are they privy to such classified information? How do they know everything they do?"

It just didn't make any sense. Even if they were "agents," something I wasn't entirely sure I believed, they wouldn't be told such important classified information. I doubted every FBI and CIA agent knew what was happening with the world and why.

Elena's voice was almost mocking when she spoke next.

"It's because of Fallon's daddy," she cooed.

"Fallon's daddy?" I repeated. I really didn't like those two words coming out of her mouth—Fallon and daddy.

"Well not technically his dad, but his uncle." Elena turned back towards the closet, scanning the numerous bags adorning the shelf. "He's the Secretary of Defense."

I blinked, unsure if I'd heard her right. Secretary of Defense? Fallon's uncle?

If that was true, then it explained a lot.

And if that was true, I was going to skin Fallon alive.

I understood the need for secrecy, but after everything

we'd been through, why hadn't they told me? My anger was primarily directed at the group leader. It was his secret and his secret alone. Like any coveted object, he chose what he wanted to do with it. Apparently, I wasn't trusted enough to be in the know of such a life-changing secret.

But Elena was.

"What are you doing anyways?" I asked, attempting to divert my attention off of Fallon and onto something else. Anything else.

Elena smirked.

"Supply run," she said. "We're heading to the mall a town over to gather supplies before we leave for California."

Two members of Elena's team, Sam and Lilly, had a boyfriend in that state. The girls were desperate to get their man back, and the team had reluctantly agreed to follow.

"Supplies? Can I come?"

I knew the guys would be pissed, and that only added fuel to the fire. But I couldn't just wait around until we decided to leave for Atlanta. I felt utterly helpless and inept. I wanted to prove myself to not only the guys, but to myself.

I would be worthy of their trust. Of that, I would make sure.

"Are you sure your babysitters will allow you to go? This isn't a twenty-person assignment. You won't be able to bring them all."

My lip thinned.

"I don't have a babysitter, and I don't need their permission," I snapped. Was I being irrational? Most definitely. Did I care? Not in the least.

I was hurting, and the only solution I could come up with was to prove myself. The team had to know I wasn't just a pretty face. I'd always been a fighter. I would kick ass and take names.

"Well then…" Elena stepped forward, two bags slung over either arm. "Welcome to the team."

~

"NO WAY IN HELL."

"Not by yourself. We'll come too."

Their reactions were better than I'd expected, meaning nobody tried to kill me. Once I'd given my spiel on how necessary it was to gather supplies, the team had agreed. Once I added that I intended to go, all hell broke loose.

Calax, ever my supporter, allowed me to go on the condition he could come with.

Allowed. And cue the mental eye roll. I wasn't a fucking child in need of their permission. I was an equal member of their team. At least in spirit.

Physically, however…

I could shoot a gun, somewhat expertly—okay, a Nerf gun, same thing—and I was also pretty handy with a bow and arrow, if I did say so myself. A knife? Not my area of expertise. I knew that the pointy end went into the body, but besides that, I preferred to stay away from the keen weapon.

Don't get me wrong. I understood why they wanted to come with me. The world was dangerous, and I was, admittedly, somewhat weaker compared to them. But I was resilient and had a will to live that spanned years.

More importantly, I needed space. For just a moment.

"I'll be fine," I insisted. I stared at each face before turning fully towards Fallon. I glowered at the man, hoping he could see all of my pent-up anger and frustration. "Let me be fucking useful for once."

His eyes softened, at least as much as his eyes could. He considered me, eyes assessing, and finally nodded. Before anyone could protest, he held up a fist.

"Would you be willing to take one of us with you?" Fallon asked. "A compromise."

A compromise.

That I could do.

"Fine," I said, and I saw Calax straighten his shoulders expectantly. Poor Callie. Did he not realize I needed a day free of boyfriends? I loved him, but he'd lied to me. Yeah. Yeah. Yeah. I probably should get over it. But I was angry, petty, and vindictive. "I choose Tam, the ninja."

"Tam?" Calax said, brows furrowing. Ryder just gaped at me.

"He's the only one I'm not pissed at. Well, I'm not mad at Asher, but I want a ninja covering my back."

Tam blushed, and I could've sworn he mumbled, "Not a ninja," beneath his breath.

Without waiting for them to respond, I stormed towards my bedroom. I wouldn't have been able to tell you what I was doing. Was I running? Hiding? We all had a tendency to run, me more than anybody. I wasn't a fighter, and my flight response nearly overwhelmed me.

My breathing was ragged, shallow almost, as I pressed my forehead against the wall. There were so many emotions inside of me at that moment, but I was unable to detangle them all. It led to a combination of hurt, anger, and disappointment. The latter emotion was aimed at myself. I wanted to be someone they could trust and count on, someone like Elena. I'd spent my life hiding in my parents' shadows, and I was desperate to snatch the first available drop of sunlight. I wanted to feel needed, a juxtaposition I didn't entirely understand. The more I thought about it, the more I corrected myself. No, I *needed* to feel needed.

The door behind me opened, and I looked up, expecting Ryder or Calax. I was pleasantly surprised to see Declan standing in the doorway.

Staring at my best friend, my heart began beating almost painfully. He stared back at me as if time and space hadn't diminished our feelings towards one another, our seemingly unbreakable friendship. He stared at me as if I still held the stars to his darkness.

But I, too, suffered from the delusion of believing that no matter what, no matter how far I drifted from a person, we would always find our way back to each other in the end.

Even in the dissonant chaos of reality.

"Are you mad?" he signed, eyes carefully surveying my face. Every twitch of my lips, every blink of my eyes, every hand gesture, I knew would be analyzed. I expected nothing less from Ducky.

"Yes. No. I don't know." I immediately turned towards one of the drawers—Calax's. He'd taken to sleeping in my room most nights.

I grabbed one of his long black shirts and the smallest pair of jeans I could find. Elena had insisted that we needed to dress as guys. Being a woman had always been dangerous, but that danger only seemed to increase with time. The world was rapidly spiraling straight into the pits of hell. All we could do was hang on for the ride.

Eyes trained on the clothing despite my face, and lips, aimed at Declan, I continued, "I don't know how I'm supposed to feel. I'm mad and upset that you guys lied to me. And I'm disappointed in myself that you guys can't trust me."

I felt him in front of me a moment before he tapped on my shoulder. I glanced up, eyes watering.

"We trust you," he signed, but I was already shaking my head.

"If you trusted me, then why did you lie to me? Why did you keep everything you knew a secret? And don't you dare say it was to protect me."

Declan stared at me helplessly, and I knew that he wasn't

able to answer that question. I also knew what his answer would be, what all of their answers would be—to protect me. I hated that they felt the need to keep me cocooned in bubble wrap and buried in obliviousness. I'd always strived to be strong, to be courageous, to be *worthy,* and I suddenly felt as if I was a timid child. In their minds, I was weak. I didn't know if that conclusion came from my gender or my background, but I would prove them wrong.

"I'm not mad…" I repeated, trailing off. I didn't know how to eloquently express what I was feeling. Declan seemed to understand that, for he merely nodded. I glanced down, towards my bag, and spoke in a whisper.

"I just want to be worthy of your love."

I would've never said those words if I knew he could hear me. They were too personal. I hadn't even admitted them to Calax or Ryder, the constant insecurity and doubt plaguing me. How long until they decided I wasn't worth such an unconventional relationship? How long until they left me for girls like Elena and Bikini?

I scrubbed at the tears welling in my eyes. I prayed Declan hadn't noticed my break in composure, but I shouldn't have been surprised when he pulled me into a hug. He noticed everything.

In his strong, familiar arms, I made a promise to myself.

I would prove myself to these men who'd slowly wormed their way into my heart.

Or I would die trying.

CHAPTER 3

RYDER

*K*itten was angry.

I'd learned long ago how to discern her different types of anger. She was a treasured book in my collection, and I was an avid reader. My favorite type was her petty anger. It was adorable when she pouted. And then there was this one—the dark one.

She was furious, and I wasn't sure if she would, or even could, forgive us. Forgive me. We'd not only lied to her, but betrayed her trust. Trust was difficult for her to give, I had come to realize. She'd lived a tough life, constantly under this pressure to be perfect, and the fact that she was willing to love and trust a demented soul like me was beyond incredible.

But of course I had to ruin it, like I ruined everything.

Pinpricks of fear ran up and down my spine. I didn't know what I would do with myself if she decided she wanted out of this new, precarious relationship. I supposed I could love her from afar, the way she deserved to be loved.

But could I live with myself knowing I'd had her love and lost it?

My emotions ranged from self-loathing to fear.

What had this girl done to me?

She'd turned me into a romantic sap. I used to laugh when I saw men like that, men like me. I didn't believe a love like that could even exist—an all-consuming love where your entire being and happiness depended on hers. I lived for those moments when she smiled. I could sing songs forever about her laugh, though my own music failed to accurately portray such a beautiful sound. The way her face lit up when she was animated. The furrow to her brows.

Perfect.

She was the epitome of perfection.

I stared at her closed bedroom door, unable to garner the courage to knock. What if she sent me away?

Man up.

Steeling myself, I rapped my knuckles against the door. When she didn't immediately answer, I let myself in.

And froze.

She was standing beside her bed, surveying the clothing items she had set out. Her hands were on her hips, and her brown hair cascaded around her shoulders.

She was also wearing nothing but a black bra and red, lacy panties. Normally, I wasn't much for mismatched lingerie, but with her?

I could've sworn my brain malfunctioned.

All of that silky, alabaster skin on display…

My cock began to throb painfully.

"Shit," I managed to say at last. "Sorry."

"Why are you sorry?" she asked, laughter in her voice. "Did you need something?"

There were so many things I needed. So many things.

Every speech I had planned was completely forgotten. I couldn't even remember why I'd come into her room in the first place.

"I..."

She was so perfect.

So beautiful.

And she was mine.

It was that final thought that gave me the courage to surge forward, hands curving around her tiny waist. She stared up at me, eyes hooded and mouth parted. That indolent expression on her face...

I shivered, bringing a hand up to trace the curve of her cheekbones. Her lips puckered underneath my inquisitive finger, and I immediately imagined her mouth opening like that for another one of my body parts.

"I thought you were mad at me," I whispered huskily. She might've thought I was using that voice to seduce her. Hell no. That woman had me wrapped around her itty-bitty finger. It was a wonder I could even speak at all.

"Not...um...mad...um..." Her eyes were fixated on my moving finger. I felt a surge of power that it was my touch that caused such a reaction from her.

With a sly smile, I ducked my head to capture her lips with mine. She groaned beneath me immediately, hands reaching up to twine around my neck. Her body folded into mine as if it were made specifically for me. I'd thought, after what Liz did to me, that I wouldn't be able to be with a woman ever again. That bitch had broken what little hold on sanity I had left. But Addie?

All of my worries diminished just by being in her vibrant presence.

I pressed a kiss to the corner of her lips.

"I love you."

Another kiss went to her neck, arched to allow me better access. We moved, our bodies as one, until she was on the bed. Her back arched, those glorious breasts on display like my own, personal show.

"I love you."

She mewled, hands clawing at my back.

"I love you."

My hands paused when I reached her bra strap, and I waited with bated breath. Her eyes were heated when they met mine, and she gave a tiny nod of her head.

Slowly, to give her the chance to change her mind, I undid the strap with an expertise I was ashamed to have. I watched the material flutter to the ground before raising my gaze to the perfect sight before me.

I'd seen many breasts before. Never had I seen a pair so perfect.

I lowered my head to suck on her pink nipple, my other hand fondling her other breast. I swirled my tongue around the peak, enjoying the moans of pleasure she made. I could die listening to those sounds.

"I want to taste you," I whispered, kissing the crevice between both her breasts.

Her voice was breathless when she spoke next.

"What do you mean taste? Because I immediately think of cannibalism, and I'm pretty sure that's not what you mean."

I couldn't help but laugh into her chest.

Only Adelaide could say something like that with as much sincerity as she did.

"I'll show you what I mean. You can tell me to stop whenever."

She made a pleading noise in the back of her throat.

"Don't you dare stop," she hissed, and I chuckled yet again.

Putting one knee on each side of her body, I planted

kisses down her stomach, sticking my tongue into her belly button when I reached that point. She giggled, the sound musical.

Finally, I reached the waistband of her panties. My dick twitched when I realized they were the same pair she'd bought when shopping with Ronan and me.

"Don't forget you can tell me to stop," I whispered, hesitating. She merely leveled a glare in my direction.

Smirking, I gently tugged at her underwear with my teeth. Unfortunately, that process, though sexy, was too slow, and I quickly changed to pulling it down with my fingers.

Finally, *finally*, her perfect pussy was revealed to me. She was a delicious five-course meal…

…what the hell had happened to me?

Even my thoughts were cheesy, romantic movie lines.

But as my tongue attacked her mound and she squirmed underneath me, I realized it was completely worth it.

ADDIE

It was ten times better than cannibalism. Not that I had ever eaten another human, mind you, but if I had, it would've failed to replicate such a pleasurable feeling.

Okay, so I really needed to stop comparing cannibalism to having an orgasm.

But as Ryder completely destroyed me, it most definitely felt like he was eating me alive.

Licks of pleasure thrummed through my veins. I moaned, coming completely undone beneath his talented tongue. All coherent thoughts left my mind, and all I could focus on was him. His tongue. His lips. His love.

There was something empowering about having a man like Ryder on his knees for me, loving me so thoroughly.

One of my hands tangled itself in his black hair, while my other hand grabbed my breast, tweaking my nipple.

I tried to tell him that I loved him, but my mouth was incapable of releasing anything but indecipherable moans and grunts.

I closed my eyes, allowing my body to succumb to the absolute pleasure Ryder was giving me. He began to suck on my clit, and I just about died.

Was that possible?

To die of love and pleasure and lust?

I thought I would combust from the heat running rampant through my body.

I opened my closed eyelids, my hand still fondling my breasts. My eyes locked on a pair of dark ones in the doorway.

Ronan stood, silhouetted in the candlelight from the hallway. His eyes were hooded as they met mine, dark with lust, but indecision still flickered across his handsome features. I hadn't even heard the door open, and from the way Ryder devoured me, I figured he hadn't either.

I didn't know if it was because I was lost in the moment. I didn't know if it was because there was something in his expression, something that went beyond lust.

And something I no doubt reciprocated.

Still holding his eye contact, I pinched my nipple, groaning at the sharp sting.

Ronan's eyes glowed as if someone had lit a candle beneath the surface. Gaze still locked on mine, he reached into his pants and grabbed his rock-hard cock. He slowly began to stroke himself, each movement sensual, as if he was performing.

I supposed that, in a way, he was.

My thoughts were an inarticulate mess. All I could think about was the word cock. Why was it called a cock? It made me think immediately of a bird, though I didn't know why. Maybe I should refer to cocks as birds. He was stroking his...bird?

These men had destroyed me.

The way Ryder ravaged my pussy combined with watching Ronan's leisurely stroking made me come completely undone. My orgasm shattered, and I let out a scream, quickly muffled by Ryder's lips. I tasted myself as our tongues danced.

"That was..." I trailed off. I had no words to describe what we'd just done. What he'd done for me, *to* me. I glanced at the tent evident in his jeans. "I can take care of that for you."

He easily moved away from my hand, and I pouted like a child.

"This was about you, Kitten," he whispered, kissing my cheek sweetly. "I'll be fine."

My frown deepened. I didn't like that I hadn't been able to please him the way he'd pleased me. He must've seen something on my face, as he pressed another kiss to the corner of my lips.

"You need to get ready to leave. Don't worry about me. It'll go away."

"It looks painful," I muttered, eyes glazed.

He laughed in answer.

"I love you so fucking much."

He wrapped his arms around me, and I buried my head in the crook of his neck. Over his shoulder, I glanced at the doorway. The door was now closed, and I wondered if I'd imagined Ronan in the first place.

CHAPTER 4

ADDIE

"*B*e vigilant. Be smart. And always stay with Tam," Calax lectured after I appeared in the living room. The rest of the guys, including Tommy, had already dispersed—no doubt preparing for our trip to Atlanta— leaving me alone with my brooding boyfriend. Ryder had left with Ronan to steal maps and pamphlets from the local gas station. My cheeks flamed as I thought about what had transpired only moments earlier. Ryder's expert tongue inside of me. Ronan's hand slowly stroking the length of his impressive cock.

Had I been cheating?

It hadn't felt like that, but my emotions were running rampant within me. I didn't necessarily know how Ronan fit into the equation that was my love life, but I couldn't deny that he was a crucial and inevitable piece.

It was impossible to discern what Calax saw on my face.

Guilt? Lust? Pain? His expression considerably softened as his eyes grazed my features.

I opened my mouth to confess God only knew what but was silenced by a calloused finger against my lips.

"I know, baby girl," he said softly. My eyelids fluttered rapidly, both at his addicting touch and his words.

"W-What?" I finally managed to sputter out. He removed his finger from my lips and wrapped his other arm around my waist. I could've melted at the warmth he emitted. I was close to him, but suddenly, I wanted to be even *closer*, both mentally and physically.

"It's okay if you did stuff with Ryder." Despite the accepting words, his jaw ground together. "I don't want to hear about it, but I understand. He's your boyfriend too."

Guilt instantly consumed me.

What the hell was wrong with me? I had two amazing boyfriends, and yet my traitorous body still responded to the other members of his team. My guilt was washed away by self-loathing, nearly as staggering. I found that I couldn't breathe as both disgust in myself and guilt at my actions battled for dominance. As before, Calax read my face easily. His thumb traced my cheekbones and brushed lightly over my parted lips.

"And it's okay if it's not just with us," he said softly. Carefully. His brow was furrowed as he considered his words.

Horrified, I glanced up at him. "Do you want me to have sex with other people?"

Like a prostitute?

Before the thought could fully form, Calax was shaking his head.

"No." He ran a trembling hand through his hair in agitation. "I suck at explaining. Okay, look, baby... I know for a fact that Ryder and I aren't the only people who have feelings for you. And I also know that we're not the only two whom you have feelings for."

I was afraid to admit that I squealed like a pig.

Feelings? For more than just Ryder and Calax? Puh-lease.

And yet...

All I managed to do was gape at him like a raving, albeit cute, lunatic. Calax smiled at the disbelief evident on my face before leaning forward to press a kiss on my forehead.

My forehead. Not my lips.

Did that mean I was in girlfriend timeout? Would it involve a spanking? Not that I was against it or anything...

"These men are my brothers," he continued. His breath blew across my forehead, and delicious tremors vibrated down my spine. "And I want them to be happy. I want *you* to be happy." He paused to tenderly brush a strand of hair behind my ear. "Do you understand what I'm saying?"

"That you don't want to spank me?" I blurted. "I'm not exactly clear on the whole spanking thing."

A thousand emotions flitted across his face in a span of seconds.

"Where the fuck did you get spanking from?"

"Like bare-handed? Or with a paddle? Usually, I wouldn't be down for it because of my past, but I trust you."

He blinked furiously before rubbing a hand down his face.

"No," he said through gritted teeth. "There will be no spankings." His voice fumbled over that final word.

"Then why do you have such a raging boner?" I asked innocently.

Because the hardness pressing into my stomach definitely contradicted his words.

"Tam!" Calax bellowed, pulling away from me as if I were acid. I tried not to be hurt, tried not to feel as if he were somehow rejecting me. "Don't look at me like that, baby," he pleaded. "God, the things I want to do to you..."

"Spanking?"

I couldn't deny the heat in his eyes. An almost voracious hunger, both primal and carnal. Before he could respond, however, Tam appeared, shrugging a backpack over his broad shoulders. His eyes flickered from my burning cheeks to Calax's lustful, if not slightly glazed, stare. His own cheeks turned crimson, and he ducked his head.

"You ready to go?" he mumbled behind his disheveled brown curls. Peeling my attention away from Calax, a surprisingly difficult feat, I saluted Tam.

"Yes, sir."

And now *Tamson* has a mother-effing boner. I wondered if it was the "yes" or the "sir." Or both. I couldn't understand what had warranted such a strong reaction.

Before I could inquire, Calax wrapped his arms around me from behind and kissed the top of my head.

"I love you," he whispered in my ear, quiet enough that even Tam couldn't hear him. I was fine with that. This conversation was between Calax and myself. Nobody else was privy to it.

"Love you more," I responded, just as softly. I would never get tired of saying those words, words that I'd neglected speaking for so long. My entire life, I didn't think they could possibly apply to me. I was a broken, discarded toy, undeserving of being loved and loving someone in return. Through my relationship with Calax and then Ryder, I was beginning to realize that I was a work in progress instead of something incapable of being mended. Time had chipped away at my innocence but not my capacity to love. Maybe, just maybe, I could make myself whole once more.

Calax reluctantly released me, and I skipped over to where Tam stood, linking my arm through his. He glanced up, shocked at my instigation of contact, before once again focusing his attention on the floor. Following the direction of his gaze, I tried to note if there was anything particularly exciting about this swath of carpeting. Not even a fucking blood stain.

Such a disappointment.

"I'll see you later, Calla-gator," I quipped. I'd expected him to crack a smile—after all, my jokes were amazing—but he instead leveled serious eyes in my direction.

"Please be careful," he said. His hands clenched and then unclenched at his sides as if he wanted to grab me and make a run for it. "And come back to me."

I understood where he was coming from. Fear. It was nearly as strong of an emotion as guilt. There were a lot of things that Calax feared, the biggest one being losing me. The mere thought of anything happening to any of these men made me nauseous. Hell would freeze over before a single hair was harmed on their big heads. So I understood it. He would always fear for my well-being in this new world, just as I would his.

"Always," I responded. And I would. Somehow, someway, we would find our way back to each other again. The alternative was too inconceivable to even consider.

Arm still linked with Tam's, I hurried into the foyer. I had a feeling that my carefully constructed resolve would crumble if I had to spend another second looking into Calax's anxious eyes.

Passing a mirror on the wall, I paused to consider myself. I was wearing a baggy shirt, courtesy of Calax, and ripped jeans. My brown hair was tucked away inside of a baseball cap. Though my features were still undeniably feminine, even I had to admit that the disguise was good. From a distance, I could be just another man.

"You'll be fine," Tam whispered. "I'll be there to protect you."

With any of the others, I might've scoffed at the notion that I needed protection. I hated the fact that they thought of me as somehow lesser, and I hated that I was restricted to the sidelines when I wanted nothing more than to defend what I perceived as mine. The guys? My twisted brain had claimed them all.

However, there was nothing but sincerity in Tam's voice. It practically oozed from him in waves, an innate comfort that only Tam was capable of evoking from me. I had no doubt that he would throw himself in front of a blade if the need arose. The mere thought of him getting hurt at my expense made my stomach churn with a leaden, miserable feeling. The strength of my conviction frightened me, my heart racing in tandem to the swirling of my thoughts.

"Are you guys coming?" my friend Samantha called from where she was perched on the hood of the car. Like me, she was dressed completely in men's clothing. I felt a pang akin to jealousy when I recognized the shirt as belonging to Asher, but I immediately quelled such a ridiculous response. It was just clothes.

Just clothes.

But when Elena appeared from the passenger side, Ronan's white tank top and jacket covering her ample breasts, I saw red.

Tam, oblivious to my inner turmoil, gave my shoulder a reassuring squeeze.

"Let's go and get back before Calax murders everyone."

I had the distinct feeling that he wasn't joking.

CHAPTER 5

ADDIE

*T*he car ride was silent.

Not awkward. Just silent.

I would've almost described the silence as companionable, my cheek pressed against the car window and my thigh only inches, if not centimeters, from Tam's. The heat he emitted was almost palpable, a physical entity I longed to snatch and make my own. There was something about my shy ninja warrior that called to me in a different way than the others. The smile on his face that I yearned to see more often. The rapid flutter of his long lashes. The blush tinting his cheeks.

Confused by my own thoughts, I focused instead on the world passing before us. The procession of cars consisted of Elena and Bikini in a Jeep ahead of us, and Lilly and Sam in the van behind us. Tam and I rode with two girls whose names I'd already forgotten. At first, they'd attempted to engage us—read as Tam—in conversation before quickly dismissing us in favor of gossip. Of what they could be gossiping about when the only girls around were their team members and me...

Oh wait.

The landscape changed quickly from cypress trees to industrial towns. There was nothing noticeably uncanny about the town, no peeling paint or chipped sidings or vandalism, but it just felt *wrong* the second our cars pulled into it. I quickly discerned that I felt this way because it was empty. No moms pushing strollers down the streets. No businessmen hurrying towards their nine o'clock meeting. The lack of both people and sound brought goosebumps to my flesh. Fear, a tangible manifestation, churned low in my stomach.

My hand instinctively rested on Tam's knee, gripping so hard, I had no doubt it would leave a bruise. He glanced at me out of the corner of his eye, expression unreadable.

Without breaking eye contact, he pulled something out of his jacket pocket. The waning sunlight caught the keen tip of a knife.

"Use it," Tam whispered. "If we get separated, don't be afraid to use it. Pointy end goes into flesh. Got it?"

His expression was uncharacteristically grave. My stomach twisted even further, tightening in tandem to my hand still on his knee.

I tried for humor, my go-to defense mechanism. "Pointy end in flesh. Got it. Shouldn't be too hard, right?"

Flashing him a smile that he didn't reciprocate, I swiveled back towards the window. It was cold for this time of year, and my breath fogged the glass.

It was only then that I saw her. Him. It. The pronoun was inconsequential. All I could focus on was the gruesome sight before me, something pulled straight out of a horror movie.

There was a body lying on the side of the road—what was

left of a body, anyway. Its face was distorted, blood and bruises making the face entirely unrecognizable. Sitting on its chest, was a girl. At least, I assumed it was a girl. She had cascading blonde hair, nearly down to her feet, and wore a tattered purple dress. Her face, however, was contorted into a deranged, almost maniacal, smile. Black lines marred her skin, twisting and convulsing with each of her erratic movements. And her hands...they were curled into claws as she tore at the dead human's face. Neck. Chest.

Blood.

Dripping in rivulets down his body and running into the rain drain.

A strangled sob escaped my throat, and Tam's hands landed on my shoulders, twisting me away from the horrific scene.

"Don't look."

I went to Tam willingly, my arms wrapping around his shoulders and my face burrowing into his neck. He stiffened at first, muscles rigid, before relaxing against me. His arms tightened further, and I was greeted with the heavenly scent that was uniquely Tamson's—something almost sweet, like sun-soaked honey.

His hands rubbed soothing circles into my back.

"Shh," he whispered. "Shh. It's okay. You're okay. I won't let anything bad happen to you."

The chatter up front diminished completely once the first word had escaped Tam's lips. Normally, I would've felt self-conscious, but I couldn't bring myself to care. I needed the comfort he was willing to provide me.

After a moment of relishing in his embrace, I attempted to pull back. His hands immediately touched the back of my head, securing me more firmly against him. He gently massaged my scalp, his hand tantalizingly soft.

"Don't look yet," he breathed into my ear. My body

responded to the sound instantly. Goosebumps that had nothing to do with my initial fear pebbled on my skin.

I heeded his warning, my eyes fixed firmly on a freckle visible on his neck. I could still hear, however, even though the sounds were muffled through the car.

Cries. Screams.

Fists pounding against the windows. Begging for sanctuary. Food. Clothes. I couldn't distinguish between the cries of the ragers and the cries of normal humans.

The girl driving let out a curse.

"Shit! This is really getting out of hand."

Tam squeezed me as if he wanted our bodies to physically meld into one another. I tried to lift my head marginally, if only to glimpse the town over his shoulder, but his hold restrained me.

"Trust me. You don't want to see this."

And I trusted him. There were only so many things I could endure, so many things I could witness, before I completely fell to shreds. Despite his shoulder obscuring my vision, I had a good idea of what I would find in the once quiet town.

Ragers.

Survivors.

Dead bodies.

Blood.

So much blood.

My mind mentally depicted images of what could be happening behind my closed eyelids, each one more vivid than the last. I didn't know if I would be able to handle any more death.

God, I was so stupid. Why did I believe I would be capable of handling this by myself? Why did I think myself to be strong when I wanted nothing more than to be weak? I wasn't a fighter, and I didn't think I ever would be. Trembling in Tam's sturdy arms, I felt young and forlorn. Nothing more than a vulnerable child kicked out of the house and forced to face the world on her own.

It could've been hours. It could've been minutes. Time seemed to drag. I felt as if I were teetering on a pinnacle of discovery. All I had to do was open my eyes. Look...

Tam's warning flashed through my head.

No.

Don't look.

I couldn't decide if that made me weak or smart.

Finally, Tam's unrelenting grip on me loosened. He reached for my baseball cap lying on the car seat beside me.

"We're here," he said softly. And, surprising me even further, he pressed his lips to my forehead. The chaste gesture caused my body to shiver instinctively. I couldn't help but lean further into his embrace, even as he pulled away.

Reluctantly, I removed myself from his lap and faced the unremarkable building before us. It appeared to be a super store, though I didn't recognize the name. There were a few cars in the parking lot, but overall, the place looked deserted. A few white painted signs indicated that there was a grocery section, a technology section, a pharmacy, and even an area specifically designed to sell top-notch camping gear.

"I thought we were going to the mall," I said to no one in particular. I twisted my hair around my wrist before shoving it all into the cap. One of the girls from the front—I really should remember her name—spun around to face me. Unlike the others, she didn't regard me with distaste, merely curiosity.

"This is a hidden gem," she explained. "Everyone knows about the mall. It'll be too crowded...too dangerous. Only the locals know about this beauty."

I frowned, resisting the urge to interrogate her further.

Honestly, I was confused, though that wasn't necessarily a surprise. I tended to get confused a lot. Did it make me a masochist if I admitted I was a too-stupid-to-live type of heroine?

Why would it be dangerous if there were other people? Wouldn't we all want to band together?

I supposed it stemmed down to human nature and whether humans were inherently good or bad. My knowledge of the subject matter was extremely biased. Experience after experience had led me to the conclusion that humans were evil, diabolical beings.

On second thought, I totally understood why they didn't want to involve themselves with others.

"Pointy end," Tamson muttered under his breath. He reached across the leather seat to squeeze my hand. Butterflies fluttered in my stomach for two entirely different reasons.

Fear.

And something else.

"Pointy end," I agreed.

With a shaky breath, I exited the car.

CHAPTER 6

RONAN

*T*he last newspaper was printed a month ago. Scanning the words quickly, I deduced that people were as idiotic then as they were now.

Zombies.

Viruses.

And earthquakes.

Oh my!

The president had officially declared a state of emergency. According to the article, similar phenomena were occurring across the globe. The faded paper included a diminutive image of a town completely cleaved apart after an earthquake destroyed half the city. Another picture showed two tornados leaning towards one another as if in a romantic dance.

Fuck.

It was official—the world was ending.

Or had already ended, depending how you wanted to look at it.

Ryder materialized beside me suddenly, a handful of maps and brochures in his arms. It was something that was often overlooked in movies and TV shows. We relied so often on technology and electronics that nobody ever considered what would happen if we no longer had them. They were something we'd taken for granted, myself included, to the point that it was almost inconceivable to imagine a world without them in it. But it was important to know where we were going, which places we would stop at, and the safest routes to take.

Survival 101—learn how to read a fucking map.

"You ready to go?" Ryder asked.

"We need to wait for…"

I trailed off as Tommy exited the bathroom, wiping his hands on his pants. His eyes narrowed into thin slits when he caught me staring at him.

"What are you looking at, Ass Hat?" he snapped.

Ass Hat?

The kid really hated me. Honestly, I couldn't understand why he decided to go with us and not his hero, Fallon. But the little shit insisted on traveling to the rest area and then the gas station with Ryder and I instead of the grocery store with the others. There was something in his penetrating gaze, something I would almost describe as *knowing*.

His words had been, "I need to keep an eye on my son-in-laws."

What the fuck of the fuckity fuck?

I wasn't one for swearing, but seriously. Fuck.

I wondered if Tommy knew what I knew—that Addie wasn't only dating Calax. She hadn't realized I'd been nearby the day she returned from that bitch Liz's house. Calax and

Ryder had both told her that they loved her, and then they'd decided to become one big happy family.

Without me.

But then...

My body turned to flames as I envisioned her the last time I saw her. God, I hadn't been able to think of anything else. That vision was on a loop in my head. Over and over again, each one bringing me to the highest peak of pleasure.

Her brown hair cascading over her shoulders.

Her pink lips parted, a breathy moan escaping.

Her tits bouncing as she rocked her hips, each nipple sharp and beaded and just begging for attention.

Damn that woman.

It was impossible for me to think of anything or anyone else.

"I just took a monster shit," Tommy shared helpfully. Ryder pinched the bridge of his nose.

"How interesting," he said through gritted teeth.

Tommy's eyes narrowed even further. They looked like pinprick orbs behind his thick glasses.

"You're supposed to be nice to me. That's the bro rule. I read the rule book. I have the soundtrack. I effing invented the Broadway musical."

"There's a Broadway musical?" Ryder stage-whispered to me.

"At least he's cutting down on the swearing."

Fallon had gotten on his ass more than once for his crude language. He had called it "barbarian," which was hypocritical because Fallon himself swore like a sailor.

"Suck a motherfucking dick, RyRy," Tommy snapped, and Ryder bristled at the use of Addie's nickname for him. I had to agree—it did not hold the same appeal coming out of a young psychopath's mouth.

Without waiting for a response, Tommy shouldered past us and headed to where we'd parked the Jeep.

"I get shotgun!" I yelled to the tiny devil.

Tommy merely gave me the finger and said, "I licked it, so it's mine!" Silence. "Bitch!"

I watched him go with a chuckle and a small shake of my head. Tommy was definitely a strange little man. I supposed that was why Addie and him got along so well.

"Why do we put up with him again?" Ryder asked from beside me.

"Because Addie loves him and we love her, so by default, we have to tolerate the little shit." I crossed my arms over my chest as I watched Tommy pointedly rub his ass against the passenger side door, as if he was staking his claim.

"Love?" parroted Ryder, eyebrow quirking.

I frowned. The words I'd said earlier played in my head on repeat.

We love her.

We love her.

Shit.

"I meant...like a friend. Of course." I let out a breath of laughter, rubbing a hand through my green-tipped hair.

My brother eyed me with an inquisitive raise to his brow. His eyes—a burnt amber color two shades darker than my own—seemed to see me more clearly than I saw myself.

Sometimes, it was difficult to believe he was my brother. I'd been alone for so long that the prospect of having a family eluded me. Even now, staring at his face with striking similarities to my own, it felt completely surreal.

But I knew my brother's expressions as well as I knew my own.

"Friend," he said dryly.

"Friend."

"Who are you lying to?" he continued. "Me or yourself?"

I didn't understand what he meant. Did he know about my feelings for her? No, he couldn't have. I kept them safely hidden under lock and key.

Ryder's words, however, filled me with an almost incandescent fury. My hands clenched into fists as I resisted the urge to punch him in his smug face.

"Oh please. You're one to fucking talk. I know that you're with Addie also. I know that you share her with Calax. How does that work? Do you get her on alternating weekends? Is it a joint-custody agreement?" Laughing humorlessly, I took a step closer to Ryder and jabbed a finger into his chest. "I'm surprised that you, of all people, are willing to be in a relationship. How long until you get bored of her? I'm honestly surprised you lasted this long and didn't cheat—"

Before I could finish my thought, Ryder exploded. That was the only word I could think to describe it. One second, he was mere inches in front of me, trembling with unsuppressed rage, and the next, he was on top of me, leveling punch after punch to my face.

"Don't talk about her like that," he seethed between blows. "I." Punch. "Love." Punch. "Her."

Breathing heavily, he rolled onto his back. My face ached something fierce, but I knew I deserved it. I didn't know what had possessed me to say what I had, only that I regretted it immediately once the words left my mouth.

"You don't know shit," Ryder said after a moment, wiping spit out of the corner of his mouth.

I remained silent.

"I would never do anything to hurt her," he continued. "I love her, and I think you love her too. Hell, I know you love her. I'm not a fucking idiot."

Still, I kept my mouth pressed into a thin line.

How did one respond to that? What type of sick bastard did it make me to be in love with my brother's girl? Ryder would hate me if he discovered the extent of my feelings. It wasn't just lust I felt for the eccentric if not slightly crazy brunette, but something deeper. Something that made my stomach clench painfully whenever she was in the room. When she smiled at me?

Well...

I was a goner before I even knew her name.

"I'm not dumb. I see the way you look at her...the way everyone looks at her. And I see the way she looks back." Ryder's voice was uncharacteristically soft, and I wished I could see his face. Instead, I focused on the water stains darkening the white tiles of the ceiling. "Calax and I agreed that she's a good fit for our team. She's the missing piece we hadn't realized we needed. And that girl needs all the protection she can get. Of course, we haven't discussed it yet with the whole team—"

"What are you saying?" I asked, breaking into his speech.

But Ryder never responded. Trying to taper my annoyance, I rolled onto my elbow to face him. I paused when I noticed the predicament he'd found himself in. There was a gun aimed at his face.

Holding the gun, expression positively gleeful, was a girl about our age with blonde curls and bright blue eyes.

"Hello, boys," she purred.

I was distantly aware of someone coming up behind me. Before I could even move, something hit me on the side of the head and darkness consumed me.

ADDIE

Guy me had a distinct walk.

A sort of swagger, I would say, that included both hip

shakes and long strides. As a guy, you had to account for a lot of things. More muscles. Larger feet. And a penis.

Did a penis impact the way a guy walked? I couldn't even imagine having something hanging between my legs, swinging in the breeze.

I had to think of a guy's name.

What was a good name for a guy with an invisible, metaphysical penis? I was almost positive that there wasn't a baby name category for that.

"What are you doing?" Tamson asked me as we moved to the front entrance of the store. I attempted to lower my voice in a poor impersonation of a man's.

"Sucking titties."

Because that was what men said. Obviously.

Tam blinked, seemingly unable to decide if I was certifiably insane and needed to be committed or if he should just let me be me. He eventually decided on the latter with a slow shake of his head.

"You know you don't have to act like a guy, right?" Driver Girl said.

"But what's the fun in that?" I kept my voice low and gravelly, thumping my chest for emphasis. I immediately winced as a shooting pain reverberated through my breasts. "I'm…Antwonia."

Tam made a strange sound in the back of his throat, a combination between a gasp of disbelief and a laugh.

"Actually, I need to come up with my gangster name. Because that's a real thing we need to take into consideration. How do you feel about Lil' One Punch? I see real merit in a name like that."

Tam snorted, quickly bringing his hand up to cover his laughing mouth.

Frowning, I added in my normal voice, "Never mind. Being a guy is too hard. I only had a fake penis for a minute, and I'm already exhausted trying to keep it limp. I like tits way better." I grabbed my breasts for emphasis. "On me that is. I like penises on men."

"What is she even saying?" Driver Girl whispered to Tam. Tam shook his head at her, unable to articulate an answer, but kept his eyes trained on me. There was something almost carnal in his heated gaze. It took me a moment too long to realize I was still holding my boobs like they were a freaking life preserver. Dropping my hands to my sides, I marched into the darkened store.

"Let's go shopping, bitches!" And then, because I could, I added in a deep voice, "Let's get some shopping done, home dogs."

Nailed it.

CHAPTER 7

ADDIE

*B*eing a boy had its perks. For one, I could slap mannequins on the ass without getting weird looks. Secondly, I could caw like a bird without judgement. And finally, I could refer to Tamson as my "bro-mate" and "bro-bear." Things would've gone down differently if I was a female.

After my third bird call, Tamson rubbed at the skin between his eyes.

"You are a very strange person," he said, but there was no malice in his voice, just awe.

"The strangest," I agreed without preamble. The cutest blush curled up Tam's neck, darkening his cheeks. When he caught me staring, he quickly glanced down at the ground. His reddish-brown hair obscured his features.

"Why do you do that? Why do you hide?"

He peeked at me through his fringe of thick lashes. I'd never realized how beautiful his eyes were before. The splatter of freckles accentuated the green in his eyes and the length of his lashes.

"You're beautiful," I blurted. If it was possible, and I didn't think it was, his cheeks reddened even further. "I know it's weird, but it's true. And I don't like it when you look away. It makes me think you're sad, and I hate when you're sad."

As I spoke, I did what was instinctive—I took a step closer. His breath fanned over my face as my hand tucked a curl behind his ear. His eyes flickered from my lips to my eyes and then back to my lips.

Was he going to kiss me?

Did I want him to?

I remembered Calax's words from earlier. He told me, for lack of better words, to follow my heart. I knew that if I was to kiss him, neither Calax or Ryder would consider it cheating.

His head lowered…

"What the fuck are you two doing?" a strident voice demanded. Tamson jerked away as if he had been slapped. His eyes flickered towards the figure over my shoulder. Turning, despite already knowing who I would see, I flashed Elena a singularly beautiful smile.

"Hey, home girl," I said in my rather impressive, if I did say so myself, man voice. Her nose wrinkled in distaste.

"Whatever. Just hurry up and come help us load."

Tam, chin still touching his chest, hurried after Elena. I might've thought he was running from me if he hadn't stopped mid-step, taken a shuddering breath, and then extended a hand back towards me. For some reason, I thought that this moment was a turning point in our relationship. Something monumental, like crossing an ocean.

Heart hammering in my chest, I took his hand and followed him through the cluttered store.

∾

THERE WAS NO ELECTRICITY. Instead, we relied on the thin shaft of light from the flashlight Elena held. I knew Tam had one in his pocket as well.

I tried to tell myself it was the flashlight I felt when I had been pressed against him. Just the flashlight.

However, I completely understood. I, too, experienced the issues caused by a phantom dick. Those things were impossible to control. Seriously. Trying to tame an imaginary penis was a struggle.

The rest of the girls were convened in the camping department when we arrived, Tam's fingers interlocked with mine. A few girls, one in particular that I recognized to be either Lacey or Missy, glared at our connected hands, but when Tam didn't pull away, I didn't either. Instead, I kept an imperious set to my chin.

I was a bad bitch.

Bad…man.

Bad boy. Bad boy.

"You're singing," Tam whispered out of the corner of his mouth.

"I'm channeling my inner male criminal," I responded.

"What does that even mean?" Bikini interrupted, rather rudely, if you asked me. She wasn't privy to our private conversation.

Keeping my expression and voice serious, I said, "I stab bitches."

Tam made another one of his strange noises, and Bikini turned on her heel with a dramatic huff.

The next hour passed smoothly. We gathered camping supplies, including tents, sleeping bags, and flashlights, and what was left of the food. The pharmacy had unfortunately already been picked through. Nothing remained besides an adhesive wrap and something labeled for lessening diarrhea.

We stopped in the clothing section to grab a few outfits. I fingered the lace of a rather revealing nightgown.

"So what did you do before?" I asked Tam, who was trailing behind me. I grabbed a pair of jeans that looked to be in my size and slipped them over my arm.

"Before what?" He perused a couple of sweatshirts still left on the rack, grabbed one, held it out in front of me, and then placed it back down when he decided it wouldn't fit me.

"Before everything went to shit," I supplied.

"Well…you already know my history." He considered a large, pink zip-up sweatshirt before eventually deciding on it. He tossed it over his shoulder.

"I meant on the team. What did you do?"

He gently removed the jeans I'd grabbed from my arm, placing it on top of the sweatshirt on his shoulder.

"I went on missions. Recon, usually. Traveled the world. Went to parties." He shrugged nonchalantly, but I stopped to gape.

"You? At parties? The world really has ended." I chuckled softly, and a small smile flitted across his handsome features. My breath caught. He really was beautiful, but when he smiled, he was positively radiant.

"World ended," he mocked, tossing a pair of leggings in my face. I caught the offending fabric before shoving it back in his face.

This was a Tam I was unfamiliar with. Carefree. Joking. It was almost as if he were an entirely different person from the shy and timid one I'd grown accustomed to. The change wasn't bad…just surprising.

I spotted Bikini over Tam's shoulder, walking towards us. Despite wearing a hat and loose clothing, she was still ethereal in beauty. I couldn't ignore the self-consciousness that rippled within me, permeating the air.

"We're waiting in the cars," she stated bluntly. Her eyes flickered appreciatively over Tam, resting on his ass. He went positively rigid, expression glacial, but refused to turn around.

Without another word, Bikini hurried towards the front entrance of the store. She rewarded us with her signature hair flip, which was hilarious because her hair was hidden beneath a cap. Instead, it translated into a weird hand gesture.

Tamson met my eyes, and we both erupted into giggles. Well, I giggled like the manly man I was, and Tamson simply chuckled softly.

"Shall we go?" I asked dramatically.

Tam mimicked Bikini's hair flip with the jeans still wrapped around his shoulders.

Giggling yet again, I nudged him with my shoulder. "I like this side of you. Don't get me wrong, I like both sides of you, but you should let fun, carefree Tam come out to play more often."

As expected, he ducked his head and blushed. I couldn't help but smile at the change. I had been wrong in my initial assumption. They weren't two separate men, but one man in desperate need of confidence. I had the distinct feeling that I was only just barely scraping the surface of everything Tam could be.

The eruption of thunder made me jump. This was immediately followed by rain pelting against the vaulted roof. It came down in torrents so heavy, it was impossible to see the cars in the parking lot.

Bikini was glaring out the window, her arms crossed under her perky, perfect tits. Her per-tits, as I referred to them.

Tam frowned at the aggressive weather before gently wrapping the pink sweatshirt he had grabbed around my head. It would do little to quell the frigid air, but hopefully it would protect me from the rain.

"Are you not going to offer me one?" Bikini snapped. When Tam merely ducked his head, I pointed towards the clothing section.

"There are sweatshirts in aisle one."

She sputtered, indignant, before pushing open the doors and charging straight into the storm.

It only took a few seconds before the screaming began.

Loud, earsplitting screams. Cries of anguish. Agony. Pain. Torture.

Only a few feet away from the glass door, I could see everything. Her skin turning red as the rain relentlessly pelted down. Her hair coming out in clumps. Blood mixing with rainwater.

I immediately ran forward with a shout, but Tam put a restraining arm around my stomach, holding me back. Once I was secured behind him, he grabbed the sweatshirt off of my head and secured it over his own. My pulse was hammering.

"Be careful!" I cried, knowing and fearing what he was about to do.

Before he could exit, however, a familiar Jeep pulled up. I recognized Elena's face instantly.

Her horror-struck eyes went from Bikini's unrecognizable body to us. Indecision marred her pretty face.

"Elena!" Tam yelled. His arm wrapped around my shoulders, now pulling me with him instead of away.

I could see the moment Elena's decision was made. Guilt briefly flashed in her eyes, there and gone too quickly for me to be certain I'd gauged it correctly. Tam noticed it too.

"Elena!" he screamed, lunging forward. But her car was

already pulling away, followed quickly by the two vans. The last one happened to go right over Bikini's body, the wheel...

I vomited onto the floor.

Bikini was dead. The rain was poisonous.

And we'd been left behind.

CHAPTER 8

ADDIE

I hurled a thousand insults into the rain. Thunder continued to clap overhead, and lightning streaked across the sky like a giant spotlight being switched on. Just as quickly, the light was snatched away and darkness returned.

"Shit!" I screamed. Tam's hands still wrapped around my waist were the only thing that restrained me. My stomach clenched and tightened as I considered the body on the ground. I couldn't look away, the grotesque sight capturing and holding my attention. How could Elena just leave her teammate behind? How could she have left *us* behind?

And Lilly and Samantha. My friends. How could they have left us?

At least, I had thought they were my friends.

"It's fine, Addie. Everything be fine," Tam said, pressing his face into the back of my neck. During my struggles, the baseball cap must've fallen off, and my long hair cascaded over my shoulders. "As soon as the storm ends, we'll go to the parking lot and check to see if any of the cars are working. It'll be fine."

"Fine?" I said, scoffing in disbelief. "Tam, there are so many things that can fucking kill us if we don't have a working vehicle. Ragers. Weather. Acid rain." My body began to tremble, a stark contrast to Tam's sturdy one pressed against mine.

"Addie. Look at me. Look at me." With a whimper, I reluctantly turned to face him. He captured my face with his large hands, his eyes begging me to remain calm, to trust him and his ability to get us out of this situation. Taking a calming breath, I nodded slowly.

Yes.

He was right.

All we had to do was wait for the storm to pass, and then we could check to see if any of the cars were working. Even if none of the cars worked, we could just wait for the guys to discover we were missing and come for us.

At the thought of my guys, panic once again threatened to consume me. Shit. I knew that they were traveling as well. What if they got stuck in the storm? What if something had happened to them? My throat closed, and tears welled in my eyes at the thought. If anything were to happen to any of them, even Tommy, I would lose it.

More than I had already lost it, that was.

"You're not calm," Tam pointed out, and I couldn't stop the bark of laughter that escaped my dry lips.

No. I was most definitely *not* calm.

With a resigned sigh, I placed my head on his shoulder. He dropped to his knees, still holding me, and I followed.

And then we sat, our arms wrapped tightly around one another, as the storm continued on.

~

ASHER

I saw my first dead body when I was seven.

And I killed my first person when I was eight. Granted, the killing could be considered self-defense, but that doesn't make a difference. Once a person was dead, he stayed dead. No more breathing. No more talking. No more living.

Lights out.

You might think that by this point, I would be immune to death, but I was not. It was entirely impossible to desensitize yourself to the pungent smell wafting from a decaying corpse. To shield your eyes from the gruesome body mere inches from your blood-soaked shoes.

To see the life bleed from their eyes in tandem to the blood dripping from their wounds.

I held the knife in a light grip, not palmed or tightly grasped. It was like holding a flower with barely applied pressure to the stem. Squeeze too tightly, and the flower would die. Squeeze too lightly, and the flower would slip through your fingers. The way one held a knife was a common misconception. It should balance on the tips of your fingers in order to slice through skin cleanly. A knife was a deadly, powerful weapon, despite the apparent insignificance of its appearance.

Wiping my knife on my pants, I turned towards Fallon expectantly. His brows were furrowed as he stared at the dead body before us, thousands of emotions flickering in his normally apathetic eyes. I couldn't help but notice that not one of those emotions was regret.

"He didn't talk," I said, slipping the knife back into my waistband. I didn't need to explain—Fallon had been present for the entire interrogation.

Arms crossed over his burly chest, Fallon took a step closer to the man.

Hunter something. I didn't catch a last name. Unimpressive in appearance with dark red hair, the beginnings of a beard, and muddy brown eyes. Right then, however, his features were nearly unrecognizable. Bruises marred his face, and lines carved from my knife distorted his skin.

For a moment, I almost felt bad. The man was fucked up, his body and face entirely unrecognizable. Just as quickly, I remembered the reasons why I'd had to interrogate him, and the pity was swept away in a tidal wave of anger.

When Fallon had first instructed me to keep an eye on the house Liz previously occupied, I'd thought it would be a complete waste of my time and skills. That all changed, however, when this assface arrived. He'd come for one reason and one reason only—Adelaide.

The lion mask still sat on the ground near his tied-up feet, discarded.

Who do you work for?

What do they want with Addie?

Those were the questions I'd asked repeatedly, all of which he replied to with a stubborn shake of his head. I had to give him some credit—the man was loyal to a fault. I might've let him live if his very existence didn't threaten the life of the woman I loved.

Shame.

"What do you want to do with the body, Sarge?" I asked, and our team leader's expression turned contemplative. On some, it might've been a serene expression. On him, it just appeared terrifying.

"Throw him outside. The Ragers will take care of him."

Nodding my agreement, I hauled his heavy ass to the sliding screen door. A demented part within me sort of wished he were still alive, if only to feel the pain of Ragers tearing apart his flesh.

At least that bitch Liz got what was coming to her. There were some people that I merely hated…and some people that I wanted to see torn apart and then peed on by rabid monkeys on acid. Liz fell into the latter category.

After depositing the body, I waited for Fallon to climb into the car. My mind immediately began to wander, as it always did after an assignment.

"Why are you such a failure?"

The words were the only constant in my life. That, and the press of a boot against my stomach. Shivering on the cold basement ground, I could only look up at my father with wide eyes. He didn't seem bothered by the fact that his one and only son was staring at him with undisguised disgust and terror. No, the man was utterly oblivious to anything but his own self.

As he kicked me yet again, tears gathered in my eyes. I'd failed him. I'd failed my father.

Bad son.

Bad Asher.

All I'd ever wanted was to be good. Now, I had trouble discerning what was right and what was wrong. What was good and what was bad. Why was there no clear distinction? The world was just a fucking contradiction leaving nothing but a murky shade of gray.

Kick.

My body ached, and I curled in on myself like old, yellowing paper. I thought that if I could somehow make myself smaller, then maybe he would stop.

My eyes rested on the handle of a rusty hunting knife…

Kick.

Kick.

I was pulled from my thoughts by the driver's side door

slamming closed. Trembling, both from the suddenly chilled air and my own fear, I turned my face towards the window. Bloated, grey clouds hung low in the sky threatening rain. It was such a contrast to the sunny sky earlier this morning.

The car ride back was silent. We passed only a few Ragers, all of which ran after the car. They became bored after only a minute, resuming their endless wandering.

Ragers.

My heart hurt when I saw their distorted, grotesque faces. They'd been human once. Wives, husbands, fathers, and mothers. Children. Brothers and sisters. Now, they were nothing more than monsters.

Was that what human nature had resorted to? Was that evolution transforming us all into our true selves? The caveats of a human being were impossible to ignore. Perhaps we were all monsters. Perhaps this was a sign from God or whoever ran the universe that we were in dire need of change. Perhaps this was a punishment.

I knew that I was a monster. It was something I'd accepted long ago. Addie may have believed that I was a sweet, innocent boy, but her perception of me was wrong and tainted by situations she couldn't have possibly begun to understand. Sure, I may not have engaged in as much sexual activity as my brothers, but I was anything but innocent. My soul had long since been darkened by both my actions and my past.

Despite wanting her for myself, I knew that it could never be. I didn't want my own darkness to tarnish her vibrant light.

We didn't talk during the ride back to the house, though that was hardly surprising. I didn't think Fallon liked me very much. To be fair, the surly bastard didn't like anyone. Besides one petite female with dark brown hair.

Hell, she was the only one who'd ever made him smile.

Turning once again towards the window, I watched the fields flash by before subtly transforming into dense forests. The beginnings of rain pounded against the roof of the car. Thunder roared in the distance, the sound deafening.

"Weather's getting bad," I mused. Fallon, of course, merely grunted in response.

We pulled in front of Elena's cute Victorian manor. There were no cars currently in the driveway, a fact that made my blood turn to ice. Ryder and Ronan, at the very least, should've been back by now.

Fallon's lips twisted slightly, the only indication he was anything but impassive. His eyes roamed over the empty driveway and the darkened windows. Not one candle flickered in the house.

Clouds continued to release their torrents of rainfall, each one piercing into the roof of the car with a penetrating force. It almost felt as if the sky was crying. Falling apart, piece by piece. Tear by tear.

Fallon put the car into park, but continued to sit behind the wheel. His long fingers tapped an unfamiliar pattern, the first crack in his apathetic exterior.

"Why isn't anyone home?" he asked. Despite his question being spoken aloud, I didn't dare respond. Fallon, like Adelaide, had a tendency to speak through his thoughts. Any response from me would only serve to annoy him.

I felt immense relief. The last thing I wanted Addie to see was me, walking into the home with bloodstained clothes and a feral look in my eyes. I didn't want her to see me as someone dark and broken. No, the further I could remove her from my other identity, the happier everyone would be.

The good guy. The sweet guy. The loving guy.

I could be all of those things. Hell, I *wanted* to be all of those things.

Shaking my head to clear my muddled thoughts, I tossed open the passenger side door.

It was my hand that the rain hit first.

I let out a cuss of pain, instantly pulling myself back into the car.

"Shit. Shit. Shit."

The skin was turning red, a stark contrast to my usually pasty tone. Fallon's eyes widened as he took in my hand. Before I could say anything, he grabbed it and held it up to his face. His grip, combined with the blistering pain from the rain, was enough to make me hiss through clenched teeth. Damnit. The man didn't know the meaning of the word "gentle."

"Shit," he agreed after a moment of surveying my reddened hand. He released me as if I were toxic, and I allowed my hand to drop limply into my lap.

Shit was right.

And where were the others?

My mind conjured up images, each one more horrific than the last. Adelaide trapped outside, her skin reddening like a ripe tomato. Screams reverberating through the darkened sky, nearly overtaking the steady pound of raindrops. My brothers, lying in a pool of their own blood. Adelaide, her features nearly indistinguishable. I squeezed my eyelids shut as if that could somehow alleviate the mental anguish I felt. If anything were to happen to her, to any of my brothers, I would lose my mind. There was only so much mind I had left to lose.

Fallon's face was pinched as if he'd eaten something particularly sour. His eyes were narrowed on the door of the house. What was going through that calculating head of his? Was he willing someone, anyone, to exit? Was he envisioning Adelaide smirking at him through the window? Or, and this seemed to be the most likely option, was he planning someone's murder? Unfortunately, you weren't able to kill the weather. Shame.

Seeming to make up his mind about something, he put the car back into drive.

"What the hell are you doing?" I asked. Without bothering to respond, Fallon dropped his foot on the gas. I let out a curse as we flew over loose pebbles and broken cement. I could see the gray door of the garage looming ominously ahead of me. Closer and closer and closer...

Bracing myself for the impact, I turned my face away. The car crashed straight through the closed garage door. Glass shattered, keen shards barely missing my covered face. I felt a few lodge themselves inside of my arms, the pain barely registering over the blood roaring through my ears. My breath left me in a swooping exhale, even as my heart continued to pound erratically inside of my chest. I glanced at Fallon out of the corner of my eye. The burly bastard didn't seem to notice, or care, that he had slivers of glass in his hair and face. Bourns of blood cascaded down his face.

Without a word, Fallon climbed out of the car and stormed towards the door. I quickly scrambled after him.

I could feel his fear and worry as if it were a tangible being. It made the air almost stifling hot and sent goose-bumps racing up and down my arms.

"Adelaide!" Fallon roared, striding down the hallway. And that was the only word adequate enough to describe his tone —a roar. Hints of panic seeped through. "Adelaide!"

"What's going on?" a tired, gravelly voice mumbled from behind me.

Calax stood in the doorway of one of the spare bedrooms, his face silhouetted in shadows. Even then, I could see his sleep tousled dark hair and his massive outline. He let out a yawn, his fist coming up to block the sound.

"Where's Addie?" I asked, not wasting any time with

pleasantries. I didn't have the patience to be pleasant when her life was in danger. I thought about the dead body that I'd left to rot. No, I most definitely did not have the patience. When someone or something threatened the people I loved, I was willing to destroy the world. It would fall into shambles. Burn away.

Hell if I cared.

At the mention of her name, he stepped closer. Lightning streaked overhead, highlighting his cold face. His brow was furrowed, and his lips were turned down.

"What's going on?" he repeated.

I grabbed a flashlight out of my waistband and flipped it on. Holding it up to my red, blotchy skin, I allowed him to see for himself. For a moment, he merely looked confused. His eyes tightened, surprise giving way to confusion and annoyance. After another long second, that confusion morphed into horror.

"The rain?" he asked. Despite the fear evident in his facial expressions, his voice was devoid of any feeling. He could've been reciting a fact. I knew, from experience, that this was a defense mechanism. It was the slow churning lava before a volcanic eruption. The calm before the storm. "It did that?"

"Acid rain," I responded, nodding once in confirmation.

Calax, to some, resembled a monster. With his hulking frame and dark, intrusive eyes, he could've been one. I'd never considered him scary until that very moment. His eyes turned glacial, and his hands clenched into fists. Like Fallon, he wore an expression that only screamed one thing— murder. For the first time in all the years I'd known him, I was terrified. That, combined with my already over- whelming fear for Adelaide and my brothers, was an intense emotion. My body began to shake as both adrenaline and distress warred for dominance.

"Calax…" But he was already charging down the hall and into the kitchen.

The rain was acid.

Three of our brothers were missing.

And the woman we loved, the glue that held us all together, was facing the storm.

CHAPTER 9

ADDIE

I didn't have a lot of toys when I was younger. Besides Dolly, there wasn't a lot that I wanted. I was once caught playing with plastic cars, and DOD screamed at me for behaving like a boy. If I were to use fake medical tools I stole from the infirmary to play doctor, Mother would whack me upside the head. No reason besides the fact that she was a bitter woman. That was the reason for all abuse, I had come to realize—bitterness. It took years of therapy for me to understand that I wasn't to blame for the actions of my parents. They were the monsters, and I was the victim.

I bounced the red ball once more against the linoleum tiles. I allowed the motion to soothe me, to ease my inner turmoil. Up and down. Up and down. It was surprisingly easy to focus on the ball, only the ball, and to block out the rest of the world. Up and down. Up and down.

Tam sat behind me, his body heat almost stifling. Unlike me, his eyes were drawn to the gruesome display through the translucent window. The body. The dead girl.

The girl who'd been alive only an hour earlier.

No. I couldn't think about her. Pinpricks of terror sent my veins alight. Fear strangled me in an iron vise.

Up and down.

Bounce.

There was no word to describe the sound the ball made as it ricocheted off the white tiles. A plop, perhaps? Surely it couldn't be called a "bounce." The sound most definitely did not have that quality—

"Addie…" Tam murmured. I felt rather than saw him inch closer to me. His arms came to wrap around my waist, pulling me against his surprisingly firm and muscled chest. "You're thinking aloud again."

"Sorry," I said automatically. He rubbed his nose into my scalp.

"Don't apologize."

"Sorry."

He chuckled, his hands tightening. Despite the horrors of our situation, my heart gave a wild thump at his initiation of contact. Once again, I was reminded of the two faces of Tam —the shy, timid boy who used his hair as a shield, and the MMA fighter who exuded confidence. I didn't know what had changed within him now that we were alone, only that I liked it.

I liked *him*.

Both sides of him, that was. I liked him, and I didn't know how I felt about that.

"Why are you touching me?" I blurted before I could think my words through. I inwardly winced when Tamson's body went ramrod straight behind me, and his hands dropped from my waist. My body cried out at the loss of heat.

I didn't even have to look to know that his face would be a bright crimson and his head would be ducked down. What the hell was wrong with me? I was a verbal bullet—once I was let loose, I hurt everyone in my path. Words escaped my mouth before I could reel them back in.

"No. No. No," I said, reaching for his arms and rewrapping them back around my waist. "That's not what I meant. I just meant... Ugh. Words are hard and annoying. Why can't we just telepathically communicate? That would make things ten times easier..." I trailed off, my teeth gnawing on my lower lip. Tam, behind me, remained stiff and unresponsive. I worried that whatever progress we'd made had completely shattered by my big mouth.

I changed position so I was now facing him, still in the confines of his legs. As expected, his head was lowered and his cheeks were tinged pink. However, unlike the last few times, his eyes remained fixated on mine.

"I'm sorry I'm such an idiot," I mumbled. My hand tightened on the red ball, my fingernails leaving idents.

His lips quirked upwards.

"Stop apologizing."

"So now that we're here..." I trailed off. There was no reason for me to clarify what "here" I meant. "Tell me more about yourself."

He blinked at me, his lashes long and full. Beautiful. Framing eyes that were chips of emerald.

"I already told you," he said softly. The blush had receded from his cheeks the more I talked, and his head had gradually begun to raise. Hand trembling, he reached to tuck a strand of my curly hair behind my ear. "I lived with my grandma up until she died, and then the guys found me."

"But you never told me what your life was like between

that," I pointed out. When his expression shuttered, I hurried to add, "You don't have to tell me if you don't feel comfortable."

There I went again, fucking things up. I was the equivalent of autocorrect—you put up with me, but I pissed you off more than I helped you.

Tamson's expression turned thoughtful, almost contemplative. He grabbed my free hand and absently began to trace patterns on the sensitive skin of my palm. Goosebumps covered the entirety of my body, but the feeling was pleasant.

Amazing.

"People do desperate things when they want to survive," he said at last, voice quiet. Broken.

I thought of Elena's stricken face as she stared at her fallen comrade. That was the same girl who'd run in the rain in a futile attempt to save me. But now, it was about survival. Who survived and who died. It was apparent from her hasty retreat that she'd made her choice, and we all suffered the consequences.

But would I have behaved any differently? If I had to choose between me and a stranger?

I thought of Tommy just then. He'd sacrificed someone he loved for me, a girl he didn't know. The bond forged from that decision was stronger than anything I'd ever experienced before.

Hero. Survivor.

Was it possible to be both, or did you have to choose? Which decision was the correct one?

Tamson's finger continued to idly draw shapes into my hand. Each touch was electric.

"I did bad things, both to myself and others. It was a choice between survival and my body. My integrity. I chose survival."

Tears sprang to my eyes at his words. He'd been a kid at

the time. No kid should have to make such an impossible decision. I felt immense relief that he'd been discovered by the others, that he'd been molded into the man he was today.

"I realized something," I said quietly. One of my hands was still clenched around the ball, while my other was being stroked by Tamson's long fingers. I focused on the patterns he drew into my skin, envisioning his finger as a paintbrush.

"We went through all this shit, but look at how we turned out. We're fighters, all of us. The shit we've been through only made us stronger. I wish that my life had been different, but at the same time, I'm grateful. Who knows what type of person I would've been if I hadn't overcome all of these obstacles? Look at you! Kind, caring, strong. God, why did it take me so long to realize? I refuse to let my past chain me down. I'm so much stronger than I was before, and I will only continue to grow in my strength." As I spoke, I gained more conviction and animation. A smile broke my face apart. For so long, I'd seen myself as a victim, but I wasn't that. Not really. I was a survivor. The trials in my life may have been a burden, but my own interpretation of those events were the chains holding me back. For the first time, I felt free.

Tamson was staring at me with an unreadable expression. Before I could inquire, he closed the distance between us and kissed me.

A quick, hard kiss. Merely a whisper of what a kiss from Tam would feel like. One second, his lips were on mine, demanding and persistent, and the next, he'd scrambled away from me. His face was red, and his eyes flickered from his boots, my legs, the ball, anywhere besides my eyes.

My lips tingled from his sudden yet unexpected kiss. I wanted *more*. I wanted him. The intensity of that emotion was startling.

"Tam…" I said helplessly.

"I'll be... I'm going to look around."

Without another word, he was gone.

THERE WERE ONLY SO many times I could throw the ball against the wall. My thoughts were a whirlpool of various and contradicting thoughts and emotions. One part of me remembered the feel of Tam's lips on my own. How soft they felt. The taste of him. The other part of me felt nothing but guilt as I envisioned Calax's and Ryder's faces. And then I remembered Calax's words...

Gah. I was so confused. The more I thought about it, the more confused I became. What a shest. What a shit fest.

Between all of that, I couldn't help but feel self-conscious. Why had Tamson left so abruptly? Did he not want to kiss me? Were my feelings for him one-sided? I knew it was irrational to believe that all of the guys felt for me as I felt for them, but the wistful voice inside of me couldn't help but hope.

So stupid.

Because of your idiotic decisions, you're going to end up alone.

Wallowing in my own self-pity, I didn't notice the car until it was directly in front of the store.

I let out a squeal. They'd come for us! I knew they would, but I hadn't expected them already. I could only hope that they'd taken the necessary precautions to assure their protection. My excitement waned when four figures emerged from the car, silhouetted in the blighted sunlight.

They were all large and covered in thick, black clothing. I couldn't recall the name of such an outfit, but it looked to be military level. If anything, the rain cascaded off of their black armor.

Confusion turned into fear as they marched towards the glass door. One of them stopped at the fallen body and kicked at her chest before continuing forward. Rain continued to pelt them, though they moved as if they weren't affected in the least. Slung over their shoulders were large guns.

"Tamson!" I cried.

They were moving closer.

Black visors.

Black armor.

Black guns.

"Tamson." This was nothing more than a pathetic whimper.

Tamson materialized behind me, one hand covering my mouth and the other pulling at my waist. I went limp in his arms, allowing him to pull me farther and farther into the store.

Behind a clothes rack.

Out of sight.

I heard a door opening, followed by what I would almost describe as jovial laughter.

"Shit, man," someone exclaimed. This was followed by words too soft for me to decipher. My body trembled, and my heart hammered.

Could they hear it? My heart?

Fear pooled low in my stomach, churning the contents of my breakfast until I wanted to expel them onto the floor.

Tamson moved to drag me even farther back, and it was then that I unintentionally released the ball I had forgotten I'd been holding. The sound was deafening. Tam froze behind me.

Silence, surprisingly pronounced, charged the air like an electrical current. For a moment, I thought no one had heard the ball. I thought that I hadn't just made an idiotic mistake that could cost us both our lives. I thought that the thunder and rain had somehow masked the ball as it rolled across the white tiles.

But then, breaking through the silence, came a voice.

"Who's there? Come out, come out, wherever you are."

CHAPTER 10

ADDIE

"There's no one there, Shawn. Leave it alone," a cold voice, not belligerent but not necessarily kind, said briskly.

"You heard it, right?" the man I assumed was Shawn exclaimed. I held my breath, pressing my body even further into Tamson's. If it was physically possible, I would have merged with him right then and there until we became one person. One body. One heartbeat. I could feel his own heart pounding though his expression remained calm. For my benefit, I imagined.

"I hear the rain, dumbass," a different voice sneered. There was what sounded like flesh connecting with flesh followed immediately by a howl of pain.

"Grab what you can."

Tamson very gently squeezed my upper arm. Once he garnered my attention, he nodded towards a set of double doors that led to a separate hallway. A neon sign hanging from above announced it as the bathrooms. Nodding to show him I understood, I pulled my arm away from his. He reluctantly released me and began to stealthily move towards the desired destination. I was not as subtle as him, nor as sneaky, but I made it to the long stretch of hallway without any incident.

Tamson grabbed my arm once again, pulling me inside the nearest bathroom. The female's, I realized vaguely.

"Are you okay?" he whispered, once we were shoved inside the largest stall. He checked over my body, touch as light as a feather, for any injuries. I captured his wrist and held it gently between my two hands.

"I'm fine. They didn't see me." He let out a relieved exhale.

I couldn't bring myself to feel the same relief. All I felt was bitterness and something akin to self-loathing. Because of my clumsy fingers, they'd heard us and at least suspected that we were there.

Stupid.

Idiotic.

"Hey." Tam captured my face with both of his palms, his thumbs rubbing soothing circles into my cheekbones. "It's not your fault."

I didn't know how he'd been able to read me so easily. Was my face really the opened book he made it out to be? Or did he just know me better than I thought?

"I know," I said softly. I didn't want to talk about my mistake anymore. My mind and body felt heavy, the combination turning my legs into jelly. A leaden, miserable feeling settled heavily in my gut. I pressed my forehead against Tam's chest, and his arms, after a moment of hesitation, came to wrap around my waist. I pulled back as a sudden thought occurred to me. Tamson must've seen the panic on my face, as his hands came up to tentatively rub at my shoulders in an attempt to alleviate the pressure there.

"Please don't tell me we're going to split up," I pleaded in a harsh whisper. "I see movies. I know what happens, and the shy guy *always* dies. Always. I know I'm final girl material and everything, but I really don't want you to die. So we aren't going to split up. Promise me?"

I was aware that I was babbling, my fear manifesting itself into verbal vomit, but I couldn't make myself stop. My body trembled in his hands. All I could think about was Tamson's body lying in the parking lot, his skin melting from his face in red, blotchy streaks. Bloody tears cascaded down from his eyes. Teeth falling from his mouth, clattering against the asphalt. I closed my eyes to rid myself of such horrid images.

No. Tamson was okay. He was here, with me, and safe.

Everyone was safe.

I had to believe that.

I didn't know if he picked up on my own mental anguish or if he just knew I needed the comfort. Either way, he held me a little tighter, a little closer, a little longer. I could feel each shuddering breath reverberating through his ribcage.

It occurred to me that he was scared. Not only scared, but terrified. How could he not be? We were trapped in an unknown location with at least four hostiles only feet away from us. Guilt once again threatened to consume me.

If only I hadn't dropped that stupid ball…

If only I hadn't insisted on coming in the first place…

If only…

If only…

Those thoughts, too, were swept away in a tidal wave of anger. I couldn't focus on them. Not now. No, what I could focus on was waiting out the storm in Tamson's warm and comforting embrace.

Together.

We would face the storm together.

I cowered, turning my face against Tamson's chest and inhaling his sweet scent. It was different than Ryder's or Calax's. Something sweeter, like the man himself. I could relish in the pungent, yet wonderful, smell.

I didn't ask for much. Hell, I didn't even want much. But I could have this, right?

Right?

Just as that thought occurred to me, the bathroom door banged against the wall. Tamson tensed, his muscles flexing beneath me. I heard a boisterous laugh followed by a slew of curse words.

I held my breath, waiting.

One.

Two.

Three.

It was a trick my old therapist taught me—hold your breath when you're anxious or scared. Apparently, it had calming qualities. I didn't know for certain if I agreed with that, but just then, it seemed applicable.

My teeth bit down on my lip so tightly that I tasted blood.

Why was he here?

How did he know?

I told myself that it was merely a coincidence. Maybe he needed to take a piss. Guys pissed. My days as Lil' One Punch taught me as much. Maybe he had a baby that needed a diaper change. Thousands of scenarios danced through my head, each one more gruesome than the last. The general consensus was death. Death for Tamson and me.

He paused right outside of our stall. I could see his thick, black boots poking through the tiny crack in the bottom of the door. My heart was racing, erratic butterfly wings pattering against my ribcage and demanding release.

For a moment, the man didn't speak. He just stood there,

his presence as ominous and heavy as if he'd been screaming. Finally, after the tension was thick enough to cut through with a knife, he spoke.

"I know you're in there."

Tamson remained silent, but I felt his body shifting slightly to push me behind him. I was no longer wearing the baseball cap that hid my true identity as a female. Instead, my brown locks hung untamed down my back. I remembered Elena's words from earlier.

The world was a dangerous place for a woman, now more so than ever.

I tried to channel my inner warrior, but I was scared. And to be frank, I *wasn't* a fighter. I couldn't kick ass, no matter how much I wished differently. Instead, I had to rely on Tamson and the small dagger resting heavily in my waistband.

Stab with the pointy end.

Shouldn't be too hard.

"Are you going to come out?" the man thundered, and I flinched instinctively. The power he displayed seemed to innately command my respect. It was such a contrast to Fallon's quiet demeanor or even Ryder's eccentric presence. This was a man who knew what his place was in the world and demanded to be treated as such. "Or do I have to come in?"

～

DECLAN

The dream started off as it always did. My eyes fluttering open and facing a room with stark white walls and an overwhelming aroma of bleach. I glanced to the tiny needle protruding from my skin, leading towards a long tube. The heart monitor screen showed a steady rhythm of waves, yet no sound emitted. No beep beep beep that would normally drive me insane.

The room was utterly silent. Even with the opened door, I couldn't hear any excess noise drifting from the hallway.

Numerous flowers adorned the windowsill, a sort of demented offering. My brows furrowed, and my frown deepened. I hated flowers and the false condolences they evoked. People sent flowers to act like they gave a damn.

It was comical, really. Only one person actually gave a shit about me. At the thought, I sat up farther and glanced from the cracked open doorway to the garden of picked and artificial flowers. I strained to read the names, but none of them were familiar. Hell, one was from an Aunt Laura that I'd never met before.

And where were my parents?

My thoughts were interrupted by a figure moving in my peripheral vision. I turned, startled, to see a familiar man. His salt and peppered hair was cut short, heightening an arresting face made of chiseled bones and dark eyes. Those eyes were currently trained on me, as if his mere gaze was capable of physically penetrating my skin. I gulped at the intensity. This man was someone who was born to be feared.

Not respected. There was too much coldness in his face, his eyes, his taunting smirk.

I sat up straighter. My body ached something fierce, and I noticed, to my dismay, that my hair had been cut short. It was no longer placed into its customary braid.

The man opened his mouth and began to speak. At least, I assumed he was speaking. Instead, his lips moved and no sound emerged. I tilted my head to the side, surveying the person I knew to be Addie's father.

But his words were indistinct. On and on he talked, his hands moving more erratically and animatedly as he spoke.

When it became apparent that I couldn't hear him, a cruel smile broke upon his face. It wasn't a smile that evoked warm feelings. It wasn't a smile you should see on a man who called himself a dad. I felt my body grow cold at having such a smile directed at me.

It would be later that I understood what he had been trying to tell me—Addie hated me. She wanted nothing to do with the poor, lonely deaf boy.

The dream shifted.

I saw Addie's face, years younger, staring at me through the restaurant window. I'd dressed to impress her and her family. My father had lent me an old, black suit, and I'd brushed my long hair back.

My fingers twisted the wrapped present I'd bought her with what little money I had. It wasn't gold or silver, but it was from me to her. From a boy who loved a girl.

I wondered if she would like it. After all, a best friends necklace was beyond cliché.

And yet...

I envisioned her face as she opened it. She would be so excited! It was that thought alone that gave me the courage to march forward. Towards her.

Once again, the dream world dissipated and transformed. I was in a bedroom, the brown bedspread and clean floors indicating it as a room in Elena's house. My body was sprawled out on the bed, naked. My cock was throbbing. The feeling bordered the precarious line between pleasurable and painful.

Addie stood above my bed, an angel in the flesh. She was dressed in a lacy, black nightgown that accentuated her large breasts and tiny hips. Her brown curls hung loose down her back. God, what I wouldn't give to run my hands through them. Would they be as soft as they looked?

Eyes never leaving mine, she licked her lips, and I followed the *diminutive movement like a man possessed. She was perfect. Absolutely and almost absurdly perfect.*

She knelt down and took my cock between her plump lips. I groaned, my body arching upwards instinctively. Her tongue traced the vein running the length while her hand fondled my balls. My fingers dug into the comforter.

She alternated between long sucks and gentle kisses. I felt her everywhere.

On my cock. My lips. My chest. Teasing my nipples.

She was everywhere.

I was going to explode in her mouth. At that thought, I grabbed her hips and held her still. I wanted my cock to spill its seed over her perfect breasts. I wanted to mark her as my own—

I WOKE up to someone shaking my shoulder. The movement was so sudden that I jerked backwards as if I'd been slapped. Glaring, I turned towards the man who dared intrude on my sleep. My cock strained against my jeans.

The panic in Fallon's eyes stopped me short, and any lust I had diminished.

"Are you the only one here?" he signed, movements erratic. I'd never seen the man look so unkempt before. His long hair was out of its ponytail and hung in a disheveled heap over his shoulders.

"Just me and Calax," I replied. When he didn't immediately respond, I signed, *"What's going on?"*

"Acid rain."

Those words made my blood turn to ice. The implications.

No...

"Are they back yet? Is Addie back yet?" I signed, moving to

my feet. The wooden chair fell to the floor with my movement.

The despondency in Fallon's eyes was all the answer I needed.

Though I was worried about my brothers, I knew they were more than capable of taking care of themselves. Addie, on the other hand, was oblivious to the horrors of this world. Maybe oblivious wasn't the correct word, but naïve. She understood that there were monsters in the world, but she failed to recognize them until they were directly in front of her. She would mistake a gun for a flower until the bullet had shot through her heart and killed her. There was no distinction between black and white. Instead, she perceived the world as shades of grey.

I feared that her innocence would lead to her death.

And her death, more so than anything else, I would not be able to survive.

I'd already decided *I* wouldn't live past Atlanta. What I had to do...

Shaking my head, I focused on the three figures before me. Asher was coated in blood—not his own, I knew—and Fallon looked positively feral. He was a scary man on the best of days, but just then, he appeared murderous. A beast trapped too long in a cage.

They were talking amongst one another, but I didn't bother trying to read their lips.

Tamson was with Addie, I knew that. And he would protect her with his life. Ronan and Ryder were together. I was even worried about the little bastard, Tommy. He'd grown on me like a fungus. Granted, I didn't like the way he looked at Addie, but I reminded myself she wasn't mine in the first place. She was Calax's.

Not mine.

Fallon's head whipped towards the garage just as the door

was pushed open. Elena ran in first, her coat wet from windward rain, but her skin surprisingly unharmed. I felt nothing but relief when I saw her.

Glancing over her shoulder, I strained to spot Addie and Tam.

Lilly was there. And Samantha. And the others...wait. Not all of the others.

Fallon turned towards her and said something. I wished I could hear his words, as Elena's face paled drastically. She looked exhausted, heavy bags under her eyes and cheeks stained from what appeared to be tears.

Calax's expression contorted with an almost incandescent fury, a mirror of Asher's. Fighting off my agitation at being left in the dark, I focused on Fallon just as he pressed Elena into the wall. His hand wrapped around her throat, and her eyes widened. Samantha charged forward, but stopped when Lilly put a restraining hand on her arm.

I knew Fallon could kill Elena. And he would, too, if Addie wouldn't have seen him as a monster. The man never hesitated to kill someone if his family was in danger, male or female. It was just one of the reasons why he was the respected and feared team leader.

Noting my quirked brow, Asher hurried to sign,

"The bitch left them there to die."

My body thrummed with a blistering rage. I'd never been the type to want to hit a female, but just then, I wished my fist accidentally connected with her face. She was a petty female driven by jealousy and lust.

Fallon said something else, something that made Elena cry, before he released her. Without a word, he stormed towards the garage and the cars.

"Come on boys," Asher signed, a cheerful smile on his face. The man was a closeted psychopath. *"Rain or shine, we have to get our girl back."*

"And Ryder and Ronan?" I inquired.

"They can take care of themselves," Calax interjected. His face was glacial, almost as if it were carved from stone. I wondered what Elena had said to cause all of them to behave so aggressively.

A problem for another time, I supposed.

Right now, I had to focus on saving my girl.

CHAPTER 11

RYDER

*W*ell...

Getting held at gunpoint wasn't exactly how I'd planned to spend my day. No, I would've much preferred a repeat of today's earlier performance. The whole head-between-her-legs-as-she-moaned-my-name type of show.

Alas, the world was not so kind.

Instead of panicking as the barrel was pressed against the side of my head, I merely rolled my eyes and feigned indifference. Gun against my head? That was nothing.

So when the blonde bitch wrapped rope around my wrists and tied me against the wall, I continued to keep my face impassive. Ronan let out a string of creative curses before his sounds were muffled by a sock being shoved into his mouth. His eyes widened in disgust and horror, and he flashed them a glare that would've made any sane person piss their pants. Me? I tried to calm my erratic breathing as my mind brought me back to Liz's house.

My body, held captive beneath layers of ropes.

Her face contorted into a sneer.

Her cold lips...

I could feel the beginnings of a panic attack take root, but I quickly shoved them down. If there was one thing I learned at the academy, it was never to show fear. Fear was a reflection of your weakness, and the last thing I wanted to be was weak in front of these people. My stomach was a tumultuous mix of fear and desperation. However, anger also warred for dominance within me, and I knew that only one person, one brown-haired female, would be able to get my rage pacified.

Three girls and three boys. All similar in age. The blonde girl from earlier, two girls with dark hair, and three boys that could've been brothers. From what I garnered, the blonde girl was named Ali. The brunette was Amanda. The oldest brother, and the apparent leader, was Kai.

"I'll ask again," Kai said, leaning down so he was face to face with me. "Where are you camped out?"

Oh yeah. The assholes decided that they wanted to raid our "camp." They didn't believe me when I told them we were visitors from the deepest pits of Hell. To be fair, I wasn't lying. Elena's house was the equivalent to hell, and only Liz's house could compare.

The only good news was that they weren't killers. They didn't even want to hurt us. They were just six people playing the cards dealt to them by fate. The game was constantly changing, the rules fluctuating. One thing remained painstakingly clear—they wanted to survive.

"They're both cute," I heard Ali mumble, far enough away where she didn't believe I could hear. She glanced at me out of the corner of her eye. Amanda scoffed.

"Too dark. Not my cup of tea."

Figures. I was more of a coffee drinker myself.

The rope rubbed against my sensitive wrists, the pain increasing every second I was tied. My agitation must've been clear on my face, as Kai leaned down until his face was even closer to mine.

"Look," he said. "You obviously came from somewhere that has food, water, and other resources. I don't get why you won't just tell us. We should all stick together against those beasts."

Ronan, beside me, grunted, his words inarticulate due to the muffle. I couldn't help but snort myself. What did this man expect? To tie us up and then join us around a campfire? His idea had merit, but his execution needed some work. Bondage was more of Fallon's forte, if the rumors were true.

"Untie us," I snapped. "Maybe we'll talk after."

"Look, it's nothing personal, man." Another one of the men stepped forward, hands raised as if he were a criminal approaching a cop. He licked his lips and anxiously glanced at Kai the dick face. "We just had to protect ourselves before we talked to you. But we are sincere in our desire to join you."

This was getting fucking ridiculous. Addie was no doubt back by now and was getting worried. A worried Addie led to an insane Addie. Or at least more insane than she normally was.

A crack of thunder reverberated overhead. I'd seen the bloated storm clouds slowly inching their way to where we were. It would only be a few more moments before the sky opened up.

At a nod from Kai, the three girls pushed open the glass doors and waited outside, arms crossed over their chests.

"Stay with them," Kai ordered his brothers, and they followed. I watched in rapt fascination as Kai the dick face produced a pocket knife from his pants. It suddenly occurred to me why he'd sent them away in the first place. His hand trembled as he held the knife to my face, and in the blade, I could see my reflection.

Well shit.

He brandished the weapon with a clumsy swipe that suggested he wasn't familiar with how to properly wield it. Great. So I was going to bleed to death because some dumbass didn't know how to hold a weapon. Fucking peachy. His hand trembled as he pressed it against my neck.

"Come on, man. We have girls with us." The words were a pathetic plea.

I wanted to tell him that we did too, or at least one that mattered, but I kept my mouth shut. I had no idea what he would do with that type of leverage. Instead, I leveled an icy glare his way.

"Why don't you find an abandoned house or a store, hunker down, and live happily ever after. Have babies. Get an erection. I don't give a fuck what you do," I suggested through gritted teeth. Ronan hummed his agreement from beside me.

"Because people are savages, man. They'll try to take it from us!"

At that, I couldn't help but let out a bark of laughter. The fucking irony.

Kai must've realized how his words had been construed, as his frown deepened.

"We're not bad people," he insisted.

"No." I resisted the urge to roll my eyes. "You're just someone who holds knives to strangers' necks. Not bad people at all."

Kai's hand teetered dangerously close to an artery in my neck before he dropped the knife with a resigned sigh.

"Look, I just need to—"

I never did find out what he needed. One second, he was

talking, and the next, he let out a strangled scream as a Rager jumped on his back and bit his neck. No, not a Rager.

A fucking Tommy.

Blood coated Tommy's mouth as he released Kai, and the man fell to his knees. His hand went to cover the wound while his eyes widened eminently.

"Fucking hell, Tommy," I cursed, eyes shifting from his bloodstained mouth to the fallen leader. With a shrug, Tommy wiped his mouth with the back of his hand.

"What? I saved you, didn't I?" The little asshole raised a brow and cocked his hip to the side, daring me to disagree with him. I had the distinct feeling that he would leave me here to die if I did anything but praise his holiness.

Fortunately, Tommy grabbed the knife that had clattered to the floor and cut my bindings before I could reply. Once freed, I scrambled to Ronan and pulled the sock out of his mouth. He immediately began to gag.

"Fucking asshole," he mumbled beneath his breath, his retching turning into dramatic dry-heaving. I patted his back and held his short-cropped hair away from his face.

"There, there, sweetheart," I teased mockingly. With his hands still tied, he could do little but glare at me.

Tommy was singing softly about being the "badass of the badasses," and Kai was moaning. Besides that, and the occasional crack of thunder breaking apart the sky, it was silent.

Which was why, only seconds later, the screams broke through the silence like the crack of a whip.

≈

ADDIE

Don't panic.

I repeated those words in my head like a mantra, a chant, a prayer.

Don't panic.

I could see a dozen emotions flicker in Tam's gaze before it settled on determination. His jaw clenched so tightly, I was afraid it would break, he moved so that I was against the wall and he was in front of me. His hands pushed down on my shoulders, forcing me to my knees. Any words I wanted to say, any protests I wanted to make, were silenced by one look into his cold eyes. This wasn't the shy boy from before or even the confident man. He was a stranger, and for the first time since I'd met him, pinpricks of terror danced across my skin. My stomach plummeted at the predatory-like awareness in his gaze.

His hands moved from my shoulders and into my hair, pressing my face against the waistband of his pants.

The fuck...?

Before I could even raise an eyebrow, the bathroom door was kicked in and light from a flashlight momentarily blinded me. I flinched, immediately shifting to move to my feet, but one yank on my hair from Tam kept me on my knees before him.

Finally, Tam removed his grip with more callousness than I was used to from my sweet boy. He turned towards the newcomer, one hand moving to zip up his pants.

"Do you mind?" Tam asked coldly. I didn't recognize that voice, just as I didn't recognize his glacial expression. Was this an act?

Or was I finally getting a glimpse at the real Tamson?

I scrambled to my feet, peeking over his shoulder at the newcomer. Up close, I could see that he was entirely bedecked in black army armor. His helmet was off, revealing a strong jawline and dark hair. Wrinkles hinted that he may have been a few years older than us, but his body was the epitome of perfection, with muscles clearly accentuated through his dark clothes.

He leered in my direction, hunger dancing in his eyes.

"Who are you folks?" he asked, voice gravelly. Tam let out a bark of harsh laughter.

"She doesn't matter. I'm Tamson."

The way he dismissed me, as if I was the scum beneath his boot, brought back memories from my time with my father and mother.

The way they looked at me as if I was a disgusting insect.

The distaste in their eyes whenever I failed to meet their expectations of perfection.

The scowl on my father's face, seconds before he partook in a particularly gruesome beating.

My body tensed, and an incandescent fury filled me. After everything we'd been through…

Taking a calming breath in an attempt to pacify my rage, I looked at things logically. Tamson obviously had a plan. I had to trust him.

Trust.

Trust was following someone off a cliff with the promise that there was a net to catch you. Did I trust Tam?

As I studied his profile in the dim glow from the man's flashlight, I realized that I did. I trusted him implicitly and probably irrationally.

Lowering my head in submission, I took a tentative step forward so I was just behind his broad shoulder. Tam's hand snaked out to wrap around my waist. Possessive. Staking his claim.

"Say hi to the man," he drawled. When I didn't immediately respond, his hand came down on my ass. Not hard, despite the deafening sound, but enough to send desire straight to my core. You heard me right—desire.

What was wrong with me?

You would think that years of abuse would mean I had an aversion to that type of contact, yet all I could think about was him doing it again. And again. Maybe even harder.

"Hi," I mumbled, keeping my eyes averted. I couldn't see the man's face, but I heard his gruff laugh.

"You have that bitch wrapped around your finger," he said with what sounded like grudging respect. Admiration. Inwardly, I wanted to gag, but I managed to keep my face indifferent in response to his crude comment.

Tamson shrugged.

"Wasn't hard. Promised her protection in exchange for her obedience. Isn't that right, Flower?"

Flower? I much preferred Lil' One Punch to a name like Flower. For some reason, it evoked images of me skipping through a flower field. Yup. Totally not the badass impression I was hoping for.

"How did you know where we were?" Tam asked. He sounded both indolent and confident, as if he hadn't a care in the world. He drew me closer to him, his arms wrapping around my stomach. Creeper's eyes locked on the minuscule display of affection, desire once again making an appearance. He licked his chapped lips.

"I'm not an idiot like the others. I knew there was someone here with us." He shrugged. "Now comes the important question—what to do with the two of you?"

My body froze, and my heart pounded. I really didn't want to die now that I had so much to live for.

Tamson remained calm behind my trembling body. If anything, he relaxed even further at the man's words.

"Others? We've been wandering alone for a few days now. Maybe you could use an extra set of hands?" At his final statement, he squeezed my hips. Creeper's eyes latched onto where we connected. The way he looked at me…

Trust. I had to trust Tamson.

"Or we can make a trade," Tam continued. "I'm sure you have a bunch of supplies. Maybe even some weapons? I think we could come to an agreement."

My breathing was heavy, almost embarrassingly so. I told myself I had to trust Tamson, I had to believe in him, yet everything within me screamed at me to run. It was the fight or flight reaction I'd perfected since I was young. Tamson couldn't be serious. He had a plan. That was the only logical explanation.

Yet, as his grip tightened on my ribcage to the point of bruising, I felt the beginnings of doubt leak through my calm demeanor. The man was smiling at me, a malevolent smile that made me want to shrink in on myself. And Tamson? He was smiling back.

CHAPTER 12

ADDIE

The man led us to the same aisle where Tamson and I had initially camped out at. Our supplies, which we'd organized, were now shoved into duffle bags the assholes had brought. Three other men stood in a haphazard semicircle. When we appeared, their laughter cut off and six eyes burned a hole through my forehead. Tam's arm tightened around my waist marginally.

"Shawn," the largest one demanded. "Who are they?"

The man who had led us here, Shawn I presumed, gestured towards us vaguely.

"Tamson and his bitch."

I gritted my teeth together in a conscious effort to keep from screaming as fury ignited in my chest. Or biting. Both options were appealing.

The second man, this one with flaming red hair and dark eyes, appraised me calculatingly. The third glanced between the four of us warily. I couldn't define the expression on his face.

Shawn nudged Tamson forward, inadvertently dragging me along as well. I stumbled over my own two feet, only Tam's arm keeping me upright.

"Tell Greg what you told me," Shawn said. The largest man, Greg, raised a brow. It was surprisingly thin and delicate on his face, a contrast to his scruffy beard and mane of black hair. If I was in any other circumstance, I would've laughed. As of now, I could only hope that my word vomit wouldn't get me killed by unintentionally insulting the scary man's eyebrows.

"It's simple." Tam's calm words pulled me out of my thoughts. His body was relaxed, the underlying tension I'd seen only minutes earlier completely diminishing from his face. He looked as if he was in his element.

For the umpteenth time, panic began to take root, overwhelming even the anger. It was a diminutive seed, barely beginning to grow into a full-blown tree, but it was enough to make my body tremble. The knife in my waistband had never felt so heavy. So damning.

"You have weapons. I need weapons." He shrugged. "I want to make a trade."

Greg's eyes moved slowly from Tam's face to my own. His eyes lit up, and his gaze did a slow perusal of my body. I felt dirty under his stare, as if someone had thrown a bucket of mud over my head. I wanted nothing more than to shower and rid myself of the disgusting sensation his mere gaze evoked.

"Would be hotter if she wasn't in those man clothes," he said after a moment of silence. "Why don't we see what she looks like without them?"

For the first time, I felt Tam tense underneath me. It was

the merest flex of muscles, there and gone too quickly for me to be certain. His hand slowly moved up my ribs, to my neck, before roughly pulling my head to the side. Despite the initial sting, I didn't whimper. I wouldn't give any of them the satisfaction.

"Now now. Don't be hasty. She's still mine as of now." His nose brushed the sensitive skin of my neck, followed quickly by something wet. His tongue. It trailed down to my collarbone, alternating between tiny nips and kisses. My body instinctively leaned into his embrace. I told myself that I was acting, that I was playing a character, but I knew I was lying to myself.

"See how willing she is?" Tamson whispered, his breathing stirring my hair. His hand slowly released me, one finger at a time, and a shuddering breath escaped me. He was magnetic. It was impossible for me not to gravitate towards him.

The four men looked on with various expressions. Shawn and Greg regarded me with lust, Ginger looked annoyed, and Guy Four appeared positively horrified.

Tam slid into a lawn chair that had been brought out and pulled me into his lap.

"You know," Greg began conversationally. He too moved towards a chair opposite us. "We could just kill you and keep the bitch for ourselves."

A pounding resonated in my ears. My fingernails dug into Tam's legs. If he felt any pain from my grip, he didn't show it. Instead, he flashed Greg a cold smile. Perhaps a smirk would've been a better description. He looked positively devious and almost terrifying at that moment.

"You could," he agreed, and I mentally began berating him. You don't just tell the bad guy that he could kill you. I wasn't an expert or anything, but I was pretty sure that was a big no in the *How to Survive Psychos* handbook.

"Or…" he continued on, oblivious to my thoughts. "I can tell you where I keep my other willing ladies at. Fair trade. You get some. I get some." When the guys only looked at him, Tam nodded towards the glass door, where Bikini's body was still visible. The various cars still in the parking lot were beginning to corrode away. The paint chipped in irregular shapes, highlighting how acidic the rain actually was. How much longer until the rain broke through the roof of this store? How much longer until it made the cars unusable? I wasn't an expert on acid rain, though now I wished I'd studied it in extensive detail. That, and other natural disasters. From what I remembered during my brief course on environmental studies, acid rain impacted the immune system of an individual. It didn't burn away flesh. What exactly were we dealing with? And how would we survive an enemy we didn't understand?

All of my studies involving taxes and business law really paid off—said no one ever.

"She was one of my girls. I sent the others back a while ago, but I kept two with me for company," Tam was saying dogmatically. His hand leisurely stroked circles into my stomach through my shirt, a clear indication what he meant by the term company.

I couldn't help but feel disgusted by the way he used that dead girl as a prop for his twisted story. But at the same time, I couldn't help but note that I was still unaware of her name. Lacey, perhaps. Or Missy. One of those two.

The disgust turned inward, towards myself.

"She didn't make it," Tam said with another shrug.

Greg, surprisingly, turned towards Guy Four for confirmation.

"What do you say, Doc?"

The man anxiously fiddled with his glasses, pushing them back up his nose only to have them sink back down.

"Definitely died from the acid rain. Recently, too," Doc said. His eyes, once again, rested on my face. Unlike the lust and desire I could see swimming in the other three faces, he only regarded me with something akin to guilt and regret.

"So what do you say?" Tamson leaned back in the chair, his hand moving to my thigh. Even though the material of my pants, I could feel the heat his body emitted. His scent surrounded me.

Greg also leaned back in his chair, kicking his legs up to rest on a cooler.

"Let's make a deal."

~

FALLON

If there was one thing I'd learned from my twenty-five years of existence, it was that I wasn't allowed to kill people without a reason. Elena? She gave me a reason. The bitch had the audacity to look me in the eye and tell me that I would be better off without Adelaide. Honestly, if the others hadn't been there, I might've snapped her neck. Female or male, no one was allowed to put my team into harm's way.

No one.

My hands were clenched over the steering wheel, knuckles white, as I maneuvered our van through the car cluttered street. For the most part, the town was deserted besides the occasional Rager. It reminded me of one of those post-apocalyptic movies where everything was left behind in a state of an evacuation. Houses chipped away by vandalism and inconsistent weather. Bodies loitering the street. Cars with their doors still opened after people had left in a haste. It was a gruesome sight, a sight that made my stomach drop and tighten. The dismal nature of the town was impossible to ignore.

I had one thought and one thought only.

Protect.

Fight.

Survive.

Calax turned towards me from where he sat in the passenger seat. Asher and Declan sat in the back, identical scowls contorting their faces.

"They're fine," Calax said. His low timber spoke the words with a sort of detached quality. He sounded as if he was merely reciting a fact, not assuring me that my family was safe. An involuntary snort escaped before I could stop it.

The brooding, angry bastard was comforting me. What had the world come to?

"She's fine. I'm certain of it." This was directed at himself, as if he needed the reassurance more than I did. The man's face was tight with an undefinable emotion, and his eyes had a feral glaze to them that hinted at an underlying tension. He was unhinged, a ticking time bomb just waiting to explode. We were similar in that respect.

Tick. Tick.

Boom.

"Holy shit," Asher muttered, pulling my attention back towards the matter at hand. I followed his finger and felt my eyes widen as well.

Holy shit was right.

There were Ragers everywhere. Walking. Attacking one another. Eating the remains of numerous dead bodies. I didn't know where to look. Their skin was beginning to deteriorate in some places and melt from the bones in others. The acid rain, which had the capability to kill a grown man, did not seem to deter them. If anything, it only gave them renewed vigor. Their faces vaguely reminded me of a cone of ice cream melting on a hot summer day...a fact that sent pinpricks of aversion and fear down my spine and to the soles of my feet. I would never be able to eat ice cream again.

I'd seen a lot of shit in my life. A lot of death. But this? This was something I couldn't even begin to articulate into words. I only hoped that Tamson had shielded Adelaide from this sight the best he could. No person could face such senseless death and desolation and remain sane. My heart hammered through my ribcage as I watched a Rager, dark hair dripping down its back and black veins crawling beneath its pasty skin, bite at the neck of a different Rager. Monsters. The whole lot of them.

I wondered if this was a sign from God. Had we really fucked up so badly that he resorted to making us mindless beasts? I thought of my own transgressions.

Father, forgive me, for I have sinned.

The list was endless. Murder. Theft.

Adultery.

My self-loathing reached a pinnacle. Wave after wave of despair threatened to consume me.

I'd never believed in karma before, but my perception of life and human nature was steadily changing. Bad things happened to monsters like me. It was a miracle that I was still alive and standing.

It was a miracle that I'd been able to fall in love, though what I felt did not classify as the traditional love. I was too battle-worn and hard to feel such a mushy emotion. What I felt didn't have a name, nor was it an exact science. It just *was*. A state of being, some would say. A sensation. A need to protect.

Shaking my head to clear my muddled thoughts, I moved farther and farther away from the assembled mass of Ragers, all clawing ineffectually at the retreating car. Even from this distance, I could hear their incoherent yells and pleas.

Savages.

Monsters.

A physical representation of my inner self.

CHAPTER 13

ADDIE

I'd gotten very good at reading people. At understanding each minuscule tick in their facial features. At watching and categorizing the way they moved their hands. Bodies told a story, and a lifetime of avoiding and fearing them made me an avid reader.

Lust. Anger. Fear. Sadness. Each emotion was carefully crafted on an individual, no matter how hard they tried to hide it. The slightest tightening of eyes here. The smile brewing there. The hair flip. The clenched fist. The Adam's apple bobbing. I sometimes wondered if it would be possible to decipher a person's entire life story based solely on their expressions and gestures.

Were they abused as children?

Were they unloved?

I prided myself in my ability, in my power to see past apathetic fronts.

But Tamson? I couldn't read him.

His posture was noticeably relaxed, but at the same time, his hand was clenched into a fist. Not a tight fist, but a fist all the same. His eyes were wide and sincere, earnest almost, but his lips were pulled down. His body was an epitome of contradictions, each one prohibiting me from getting an accurate read on him.

All I could do was watch from my position in his lap as he joked and conversed with the men before us. Conversation steered from girls to sports, and from sports to lives before and after. I listened with rapt interest as they divulged their life stories. Doc, no surprise, was an actual surgeon they picked up a few days ago. According to Shawn, they were on their way to Paradise.

A place where the monsters and storms couldn't reach those inside.

A place where we no longer had to live in fear.

A place where we could not only survive, but live.

I could see curiosity pique in Tamson's eyes as he listened to their tale of the supposed holy grounds. I, too, filed the information away for later.

"So…" Greg took a long drag of his cigarette, eyes once again focusing on me. I fidgeted at the intrusiveness of his stare, and Tamson put his hands on my hips to steady me. For some undefinable reason, tiny licks of pleasure erupted where he touched me. I knew that he wasn't entirely unaffected as well, if the hardness pressing into my back was any indication. "What are your specialties?"

Specialties?

"Well, Flower here—" Tamson began, but cut off when Greg raised a fist.

"I think the girl can speak for herself."

I was suddenly aware that I had every eye on me. I met Tam's impassive gaze, and the only indication he sensed my unease was the slightest nod of his head.

Specialties.

As a sex worker.

So you see, this is where I ran into a problem. I was horrible under pressure and had a tendency to babble when at a loss for words. Verbal train wreck.

"Wow. That's a loaded question. Okay...um...I'm very good at DP. And I just learned that it's *not* a fizzy drink. Imagine my surprise when I asked for a DP and I get freaking beads shoved up my hole, and not the good hole. Who needs to prepare anyways? And why do guys even like it? What if I were to take a shit or fart while the dick was in there? It would turn into a dip-shit. Oh, and I'm also good at licking, apparently. Like if you have blue, icicle balls, I can lick them for you. And I'm—"

Tamson, who'd been pinching me to get me to shut up, finally put a hand over my mouth.

Dammit, Adelaide.

Why do you have to go and open up your big mouth?

"Well damn," Greg huffed out in a laugh. Tamson indolently draped an arm over my shoulders. The other was still wrapped snugly around my waist.

"This is why we don't have the girls talk."

Though I knew his words were for Greg's benefit, they settled in my stomach heavily. It was a statement equivalent to what my dad had always told me. Girls were made to be seen, not heard. I repeated to myself that Tamson didn't actually feel that way, that he respected my opinions and enjoyed my sometimes crazy rants. He wasn't my father. He was merely a character at this moment.

My mind, unbidden, drifted to a day only a few weeks earlier.

Ryder sprawled himself on my bed.

"Stop moving," I scolded, picking up his foot with one hand and steadily applying the nail polish with the other. I was sitting

awkwardly near the edge of the bed, the immense cast over my leg prohibiting me from getting any more comfortable.

"It tickles," he said, jerking his body yet again. I wanted to retort that nails couldn't be ticklish but held my tongue. It was a miracle he'd allowed me to paint them in the first place.

"I don't want red nails." Ronan was standing over my shoulder, watching me beautify his brother with undivided interest. I chuckled at the disgust in his voice, and my chuckling ascended into full belly laughter when he added, "I want green. Like my hair."

"Then you'll really be a leprechaun," I pointed out gleefully. It was a nickname I'd given him when we first met and one that he took to heart. The fact that he smiled almost reverently at the name now made my stomach soar.

"What about you, Tam?" I asked. Tam sat on the leather chair in the corner of my room. His hands rapidly flew over the keys on his phone, whatever he was doing holding his entire attention. "Tam!" I repeated when he didn't respond. He glanced up, startled, before setting his phone down beside him. I couldn't help but wonder who he was talking to and if it was a girl. I didn't know why jealousy bucked me like a bull at the mere thought. Pushing the feeling down, I flashed him a smile.

"Sorry." He ran a hand through his hair, the strands becoming even more bedraggled than before. He had deep bruises beneath his eyes as if he hadn't slept in days. "I got distracted."

"Texting a girl?" I teased. Did he hear the note of jealousy in my voice? At my words, his face darkened, surprise giving way to unreadability. Just as quickly, he ducked his head, and his signature blush spread up his neck.

"Tam doesn't text girls," Ryder said in a mock conspiratorial whisper. Tam's blush deepened.

"Doesn't believe they're worth his time besides a quick fuck," Ronan added. I knew that the boys were only attempting to tease him, but their words made my stomach plummet even further until *it practically fell through the floor. "He hasn't texted a girl back yet."*

Conversation veered to a storm that had hit the west coast and the cancellation of their favorite sporting game—I didn't know the difference between balls and nets and sports names. Mercifully, they didn't bring up Tamson's strange behavior.

I never did find out who he was texting. All I knew was that my phone buzzed later that night, just as the moon peeked through the boughs of trees. I turned towards the phone, believing it to be Calax or Ryder or Ronan, but was stunned to see Tamson's name blinking at me on the screen.

TAMSON: *You still up?*

I WAS PULLED out of my thoughts by Tamson's hand tangling in my hair. I groaned at the contact, pleasure warring with pain. Pleasure, unashamedly, won.

"She could be fucking beautiful if it wasn't for that scar on her face," Greg sneered, pointing to the long scar etched across my face. The blemish was the remnant of my time with Liz. Time when she tortured both me and Ryder for her own twisted pleasure and amusement. Self-consciously, I placed my hand to my cheek as if that could somehow cover the permanent scar. It was still red and raised and ugly, but it was gradually disappearing. With time, it would become nothing more than a pink mark marring my skin.

"She's perfect," Tamson snapped, the first break in his normally lackadaisical front.

Greg opened his mouth, no doubt to protest or call Tam out on his uncharacteristic, almost possessive, behavior, when a van crashed through the storefront window.

CHAPTER 14

ADDIE

*E*verything seemed to happen in slow motion. Time was suspended—seconds turned into hours and hours turned into years. I could see it all, one diminutive piece at a time. The puzzle remained blurry, and I struggled to capture and hold all of the many facets provided to me.

I saw the truck barreling through the large window, glass shattering in thousands of pieces. It reminded me, oddly, of the rain still releasing its anger on the world. The sky was falling, so it only seemed fitting that the building would fall as well.

I felt Tamson's warm body cover my own. Shielding me from the onslaught of glass particles and the wayward rain carried in by the wind.

I heard someone let out a scream of anguish, quickly muffled.

I smelled something pungent, something that assaulted

my senses. Did the rain have a smell? I would almost describe it as rotten eggs, horribly pervasive.

"Adelaide!" a familiar voice roared. I dared a peek over the top of Tamson's shoulder, stunned to see a familiar male staring at me from across the store. Fallon's normally immaculate hair was highly disarrayed. His eyes were just as desperate, as wild, as feral. The man looked positively unhinged, and an irrational surge of fear made itself known in the recesses of my mind. It was similar to how I felt when Tamson had treated me like coveted cattle.

The intensity of such an emotion frightened me, as did the lunacy of it. It took me a moment to pinpoint the origins of my fear. I didn't fear for myself, since I knew Fallon would never hurt me, but instead, I feared for everyone else in the room, Tamson included. Fallon was a lion that wasn't just out for the hunt, but for the kill. An avenging angel in the flesh.

He didn't seem to notice, or care, that wind brought in torrents of rain, burning his skin. Nor did he notice the man that had fallen, the only one without a name. He'd been closest to the window when it shattered, and the rain had begun to burn through his skin. Red, bloody streaks marred his face. With sickening satisfaction, I realized that he was still alive. The cry of pain must've come from him.

Doc was sitting nearby on the floor. He'd dived when the car arrived, barely missing being hit. Greg and Ass Face—I couldn't recall his name for the life of me—were nowhere to be seen.

The car doors were pushed open, and three more familiar figures stepped out. Asher, like Fallon, barely resembled the sweet boy I'd come to care for. His eyes were too wild, his hair too disheveled, his lips too pursed.

Calax and Declan surveyed the scene with matching expressions of distaste. After noticing I was fine, if not slightly crushed beneath Tamson's lean frame, Calax placed his hands into his pockets and drawled, "You really know how to make an entrance, Sarge."

Tamson lifted his head slowly at the voice, his eyes locking on mine. A few shards of glass hung precariously in his hair like diamond beads. Fortunately, none had reached his face, though I doubted his back had experienced the same leniency.

I couldn't help but remember the time I'd thrown myself over a body as well. Calax's body. We'd been back at the resort, and a tornado had ravished the area. He'd fallen unconscious, and it was instinctive for me to save him. To put his life above my own.

I hadn't realized before that my reasoning had been self-ish. I'd loved him, though I would've never admitted it, and it was common sense to save his life at the expense of my own. The thought of living without him was unbearable.

The fear I'd once felt towards Tamson dissolved completely as we maintained eye contact. An inexpressible emotion clogged my throat. Forgiveness. Acceptance. Something else. Something deeper.

"Let's go!" Fallon called in his standard, no-nonsense voice.

My eyes remained latched onto Tamson's as if he were my lifeline. My savior. I supposed that, in a way, he was.

Dozens of emotions flittered in his own eyes, there and gone too quickly for me to get an accurate read on.

He scrambled to his feet, reaching down and extending a hand to me. I took it with bated breath. It felt as if everything depended on this one moment. I wasn't just grabbing a hand, but something else entirely. Something inherently sweeter.

I grabbed his hand as if I were lost at sea and he were a rope, guiding me to shore. I grabbed his hand as if I were dangling thousands of miles above land and he was the only support in sight.

I held his hand, even when Greg rose, an ugly sneer on his face as he realized our betrayal.

I held his hand as he raised something—something small and black and undeniably familiar.

I held his hand as Greg pulled the trigger on the gun and a loud *pop* resonated in the air. There was no way to describe the sound. I'd heard many guns go off before, but nothing like this. It seemed to shatter my delicate senses. Correction —it seemed to shatter my delicate sensibilities.

I held his hand until suddenly…

I wasn't.

～

RYDER

There was an old book I'd found collecting dust in my foster mother's bookshelf. The spine had been creased with age, and the print and image on the cover were faded. At one point, there might have been something that resembled a dragon, but the design now favored a dark smudge against the red background. I didn't know if the book had been used excessively or not enough, though the dust was a strong indicator of the latter.

I'd asked her why she had the book. It stood out against the shiny, glossy covers and the more subdued matte designs. She waved her hand dismissively, bringing the nub of her cigarette back to her lips.

"I wrote it." That was all said with calm indifference, as if she were merely reciting that the sky was blue. A fact. I stared at the woman I'd called mom for the better part of my life.

Gray hair coiled in tight curls. Too much red lipstick. Eyeshadow that ranged from midnight black to emerald green. Larryanne wasn't a bad foster mom, as far as foster mothers could go. She was crass and impulsive, but I had the sense that she genuinely loved me. At first, I'd been bitter that Ronan had been allowed to stay with our birth mother while I'd been shipped halfway across the country, but that resentment was gone now. After all, I hadn't known he existed until he showed up at my doorway demanding money for drugs.

Larryanne wasn't my mother, but she was the closest I ever had to family at the time.

I remembered her house more vividly than any other foster family I'd lived with, mainly because it was located in the middle of fucking nowhere. The whistles of freight trains flew by one after the other for miles over prairie lands, brushing the rough, dry tips of corn stalks, filling up the blank spaces of country roads, and whistling around cold, steel silos, until they slammed against the vinyl siding of her home and into my ears. I could never sleep, due to the constant buzzing of noise.

Anyway, the woman once wore a diaper for a week because she wanted to go to a music festival and not worry about porta potties. She even robbed a restaurant once, though she'd never been caught. I imagined she wouldn't have been granted her fostering license if that little tidbit of information had become known. She was an enigma, my foster mother, but I loved her.

But her as a writer? A published author?

That was fucking hilarious.

The disbelief must've been evident on my face, for she swatted me with her hand.

"Don't give me that look, boy," she said. Smoke drifted up my nostrils from the cigarette now held between her two fingers. "I had an idea. Some characters are never able to have their stories told. I was determined to change that."

I didn't know why I thought of my dead foster mom as I stared at the bodies on the ground. My skin was red and blotchy from the rain. I'd tried to save who I could—the girls, Ali, Amanda, and No Name, as well as the two boys. But by the time I'd dragged two of them inside, the rain pounding relentlessly against my bare skin, they'd all been dead.

Dead.

Five people whose stories would never be told. Five people who had their life snuffed out in a span of a second. All I could do was stare at their blotchy, bloody skin.

One of the girls had still been alive. Only for a second, but it was enough for me to see her face twisted in agony. As I watched, helpless, the life bled from her eyes.

Kai let out a scream.

For as long as I lived, I would never forget that sound. He'd lost his brothers. His friends. Hell, maybe even his girlfriend.

If I were to lose Ronan or Addie or any of the others...

Shaking my head, I focused on the sight before me. Ronan was attempting to restrain Kai. The man was positively enraged. The timid guy who'd threatened me with a shaking hand was nowhere in sight. In his place was a prowling tiger.

"Let me save them! Let me go!" he screamed, bucking against Ronan's arms. I'd only been able to "rescue" the one who was still breathing. Still moaning. And even that word, rescue, wasn't an accurate description. She'd died, despite my efforts.

Dead.

Just like Larryanne.

Just like those characters that never had stories written about them. The side characters. The woman in the background in the movie. Everyone had a story, but only a select few were heard.

"They're dead," Ronan was saying. "If you go out there, you're just going to die as well."

"Then let me die!" Kai screamed.

I remembered the fear I'd felt when the rain first began. When the screaming began. Instinctively, I'd run outside.

My entire life has been devoted to helping people. Why would I change who I was now? I'd winced when the first droplet of rain hit my skin.

Coming to the decision quickly, I'd pulled up my hood, tugged the sleeves down until they covered my hands, and run into the damning rain. The stench of burned flesh saturated the air so intensely, I could physically taste it.

All of that effort had been for nothing. Five people, five strangers, were dead. And all I had to show for it was more scars. More pain.

More death.

Ronan decked Kai over the top of his head after a particularly brutal struggle. The man fell in an undignified heap, his head ricocheting off the tiles. When I quirked a brow at Ronan, he merely shrugged.

The rest area was silent besides the rain. Thunder crackled, the sound almost malicious, and lightning flashed in the darkening sky. Ronan came to stand beside me, eyes focused on the window as well. I didn't know if he was staring at the bodies or the sky's vivid light show.

"Do you think they're okay?" He paused, his hands snaking up to fiddle with his lip ring. It was a bad habit he'd had for as long as I knew him. That, and chewing on his nails. "Do you think she's okay?"

"Addie?" I asked. I was unsurprised that he inquired about her specifically. He was in love with her and had been for a while. Even an imbecile couldn't help but notice the wistful

glances he threw her way when he thought no one was looking. It didn't bother me, his feelings for her, just as it didn't
bother me that he wasn't the only one. Addie needed all the
protection she could get, and she more than deserved all of
the love we could offer her after having to live without it for
so long. I wanted that for her, just as long as I remained a
crucial part in it.

Besides, we'd all shared girls before. Granted, there had
never been feelings involved, but this situation was different.
The *world* was different. Conventional went right out the
window the second the first tornado had struck the resort
and an elfin girl put her life on the line for one of our own.

"Addie's fine," I said. And I believed it. She was probably
back at the house by now, getting babied by the others. She'd
more than likely threatened castration at least twice by now.
She was an innocent badass—an epitome of contradictions.

"She's a fighter," Tommy piped in, echoing my own
thoughts. His voice was subdued, no doubt traumatized by
what he'd witnessed, but the pride seeping through was
unmistakable. I'd nearly forgotten about him, but I was
grateful he was safe. The asshole was growing on me.

"As soon as the storm breaks, I can run to the car and pull
it up," Ronan said. Always self-sacrificing. I bit my lip to keep
from retorting. Now was not the time to conjure up an argu-
ment. He would risk the storm to save me, save us. I both
hated and loved him for that.

"And what about him?" Tommy asked. I didn't have to
look to know that he would be gesturing towards Kai.

Ronan and I exchanged an eloquent glance. We may not
have been brothers for long, but the bond we'd forged
surpassed years of shared childhoods.

"We bring him back with us. Let Fallon decide what to do
with him."

Fallon always knew who was friend and who was foe.

Who was a threat and who only had the potential to become a threat. A sixth sense, he called it. I had no doubt if Fallon deemed Kai as dangerous, he wouldn't hesitate to leave him for dead. Or kill him himself.

"So we wait?" Tommy asked.

I nodded stoutly. Already, I was itching to get back to Adelaide. To run my hands through her brown locks. To kiss her plump lips. To hear her talk about nonsense. To be with the woman I loved more than life itself.

Patience. I had to be patient. I was no good to Addie dead, despite the fact that I wanted to brave the storm and risk being burned to get to her.

My body throbbed at the thought, phantom pain making itself known from the many wounds on my skin. Fallon was going to shit a brick when he saw the condition I was in. Addie was going to murder me as well. Tag team murder. Who knew?

"We wait," I replied to Tommy.

CHAPTER 15

CALAX

J heard my first gunshot when I was seven.

My dad had decided I wasn't man enough for his liking and sought to remedy that. At the time, I hadn't understood what he'd meant. I watched sports, catcalled girls, and even had my first sip of alcohol. What else was connoted by that term?

He'd roughly grabbed me from my bed, hand an iron vise, and dragged me towards the rusty pickup truck already idling in the driveway.

"Today," he'd said in an imperious voice I'd learned to hate, "you will become a man."

There was something in his eyes, a sort of male smugness, that made me bristle. We drove down many twists and turns, across sweeping fields, until we parked in front of an immense forest.

I remembered being frightened by how tall the trees were. They towered over me, the sunlight just barely penetrating the darkness created by their canopies.

My father placed a calloused hand on my shoulder. He hadn't bothered to tell me where we were going, so I was still dressed in only a tank top and pajama pants. The morning air chilled my sensitive skin, and wet dew drenched the legs of my pajama bottoms. Still, I kept my chin set domineeringly high and trained my eyes straight ahead. I could be a man for my father.

I had to be.

With a loud smack of his bubblegum, he thrust something into my hands. I staggered under the unfamiliar weight, my hackles rising as I considered the long, brown object. I'd never held one before, though I'd seen Dad cleaning it out on the kitchen table occasionally.

The rest of that morning was a blur.

I vaguely recalled scrambling to keep pace with my father as he pushed branch after branch away from his face. Twigs snapped between my feet. No matter how hard I tried, my lumbering frame could not be as stealthy nor as quiet as my father's.

I remembered the doe's face seconds before he put a bullet through her head. So innocent. This was an animal unaware of the dangers plaguing the world. She merely stared at us, muscles tensed as if she was unsure whether or not she wanted to flee. I mentally begged her to.

Run, I wanted to say.

And then the gunshot...

I would never forget that sound. The way it reverberated through the forest, brushing against the needles of pine trees and into the empty burrows beneath my feet. The sound was more than just a loud boom—it was terrifying. It seemed to symbolize death. After all, what was the point of a gun if not to kill?

I thought all that as I watched Addie pause. Her hands

went to her stomach, eyes widening in shock. Blood cascaded through her fingers, staining the white of the ratty old T-shirt.

The moment that gun went off, my world stopped.

And then promptly ended.

"No," I whispered, unable to tear my eyes away. She staggered, barely kept upright by Tamson's arm.

Fallon let out a roar. A scream. A cry of anguish. Before I could even blink, the man with the gun was dead. I wouldn't have been able to tell you what killed him. A knife? An arrow? Another gun?

Tamson was running towards us, Addie held tightly in his arms. Blood. So much blood.

And when her eyes met mine, I once again thought of that deer. *Doe eyes*, I thought somewhat incoherently. They shone with an inner radiance and light that had always been able to soothe the darkest recesses of my mind. In her eyes, now, I saw something else, something akin to acceptance.

The truth hit me like a freight train. I would've preferred that, would've preferred anything besides this unbearable pain as my heart shattered into thousands of pieces. I knew my mind would soon follow.

She was dying.

The girl I loved, my reason for living, was dying. And from the shuddering breath escaping her bloodstained lips and serene expression, I realized that she knew it as well. She knew it, and she accepted it. The fight had already drained from her body.

"Grab him!" Tamson was screaming. "Grab him!"

I didn't understand what he was saying, what he meant. I had a singular focus, and that focus was on the girl still bleeding in his arms.

Asher, thank God, must've understood what Tamson was

talking about, as he lunged for an unfamiliar male and roughly shoved him into the back of the van.

It was that movement that spurred me back into action.

No. No. No.

"Baby," I cried, following both her and Tamson into the van. He placed her gently down, using a backpack as a makeshift pillow. His shirt was off and pressed against her open wound.

Dimly, I was aware of the car speeding away, jostling us.

"Be fucking careful!" That was Asher.

"Fix her," Tamson sneered, eyes beseeching. He had a gun out and aimed at the unknown man.

"I don't have the proper supplies," he placated, hands held up as if he were fending off a dangerous criminal. I supposed that, in a way, he was. There was nothing more dangerous than a man in love. We were desperate. Our tiny hold on humanity had snapped the second that bullet pierced Adelaide's stomach, and our instincts now reverted back to those of cavemen.

Protect.

I grabbed her cold hand in both of mine.

"You're going to be okay, baby girl. You're going to be okay."

My hand trembling, I brushed her hair away from her cheek. She let out a pained gasp, blood trickling in the corner of her mouth.

"You can't give up, baby. You need to fight. You need to fight, baby girl."

Her hand was so cold, it almost felt as if I was holding an icicle.

Please be okay. Please be okay.

I'd never been an overly religious person, but just then, I sent a silent prayer, a silent plea, up to the heavens. I would give anything for her to remain alive.

I'd made so many mistakes, but if she lived, I would strive to become a better person. I would fucking save the world. My soul? It was already lost without her. So if the goddamn devil himself wanted a sliver of it, I would happily offer it up on a silver platter.

I couldn't—I *wouldn't* lose her.

But when had God ever listened to me?

ADDIE

The kitchen was bustling with activity when I arrived. I spotted Asher first, flipping pancakes on the stove. He was shirtless, his abs accentuated by a light splatter of golden hair dipping down his delectable V. An apron was around his waist, and he hummed a tune beneath his breath.

"Hey, handsome," I said, sneaking up behind him and wrapping my arms around his waist. He startled, a reaction I was beginning to realize was common with these men, but instantly relaxed when he realized it was me. His hand dropped the spatula to hold both of mine, still around him.

"Hey, beautiful."

I nuzzled his back, inhaling the scent that was uniquely Asher's. Copper, almost. Like blood.

"It smells delicious." I inhaled deeply. "And I'm not just talking about the food."

"That was horribly cheesy," Calax drawled from where he sat at the table, sipping his coffee. I'd never understood his love for that dark liquid. Sure, I was a coffee drinker myself, but I always needed to add milk and sugar.

I crinkled my nose, and he merely smirked, bringing the cup back to his lips and taking a long sip. Damn. The way his lip connected with that rim…

THE STORM WE FACE | 127

I never thought the act of drinking coffee could be seductive, but I never had seven boyfriends before.

"Quit eye-humping Calax, Kitten," Ryder said, gracefully moving into the kitchen. He offered me a chaste kiss on the cheek before sitting down across from Calax, next to Ronan. It was Ronan that turned towards me, his standard white tank top boasting the intricately designed white unicorn.

"You can eye-hump me anytime." He wiggled his eyebrows suggestively, and I giggled, releasing Asher to perch on his lap. His hands immediately wrapped around my waist.

"Is breakfast ready?" Tamson ducked into the kitchen, Fallon and Declan directly behind him. All three men stopped and kissed my forehead, my cheek, my lips. I was surrounded by their love, as soft and as soothing as a moth's wing caressing my spine. I'd never realized it was possible to feel such an emotion. This elation. This happiness that surpassed anything I'd ever felt before.

All I'd ever wanted was to be loved and to love someone back. With them, I had everything I ever wanted. For years, I was told I was undeserving of love. The mere aspect of it was an elusive fantasy, a fairy tale that was whispered in the dead of night. When my parents talked about their own relationship, I'd begun to believe that love was a horror story.

And now?

Now, my entire mentality had changed.

God, I was one of those girls in a romance movie—a swooning, drooling heroine. Was that what love did to a person? I found that I didn't care.

I needed more. I needed *all* of the love.

Overcome with emotion, I turned to meet the eyes of each of my men.

Calax, the first man who'd stolen my heart. The enemy

who became my lover. He saw my walls as a challenge to overcome, not as a stop sign.

Declan, my childhood best friend. The person who saw beyond the front I built around myself. The man who loved me unconditionally, despite the years that had passed.

Fallon, the brooding team leader. He hid behind an apathetic front, but those little moments when his eyes softened or his hand played with my hair demoted him from intimidating to approachable.

Ryder, my flirty boyfriend. We'd forged a bond that others couldn't even begin to comprehend. An unbreakable bond made entirely of steel—steel that was forged from shared trauma.

Ronan, the man who hid his pain behind a wide smile. The man who forced a laugh when I knew he wanted nothing more than to cry. He had the world pressing down on his shoulders, and that pressure repeatedly threatened to bury him alive. He didn't know how strong he actually was.

Asher, my sweet friend. My confidant. My attentive lover. He regarded me as if I held the moon in my hands. Would I ever be worthy of his unconditional, irrevocable love?

And finally, Tamson. The man that was two sides of the same coin. Shy and timid. Assertive and confident. Our relationship was built on trust. And I did trust him. Both sides of him.

"I love you," I said, my throat clogging. "I love you all."

"We love you too," Fallon said, speaking for the group. I knew he was telling the truth. Love emitted from their smiles, their warm eyes, the very pores of their bodies. I could die of contentment, surrounded by the men I loved and who, for some reason, loved me in return.

Movement over Calax's shoulder captured my attention. My eyes widened as a familiar figure glided into the room. I glanced anxiously from face to face, but no one seemed to notice anything out of the ordinary.

Ryder was throwing food at Ronan, and Calax was teasing Asher good-naturedly. Normal. Everything appeared normal, at least on the surface.

But...

The girl had brown, chestnut hair that cascaded down her shoulders. Her eyes were trained on mine, an unreadable expression darkening her features.

"Who are you?" I whispered. The men faded away until only she remained. Only *I* remained.

"You have to choose." The girl—the girl with an uncanny resemblance to me—took a step forward.

"Choose?" I parroted mechanically.

"You have to choose. Live. Or die."

CHAPTER 16

ADDIE

I had an extremely slap-able face. It was funny the things you noticed about yourself when you should've been focused on anything else.

Full bottom lip. High cheekbones. Chiseled jawline. Brown curls framing a cherubic face. She wore a hi-low black dress that dipped low, revealing a swath of golden skin and considerable cleavage. A white collar and matching white cufflinks provided much needed elegance to the scantily-clad attire. At least, those were my mother's words the first time I'd worn it. A simple pearl necklace completed the outfit. There were no scars distorting her face. No bruises.

No pain.

The contentment radiating from her like warm sun beams was almost tangible.

God, I really did look annoying. It was no wonder Elena wanted to punch me. Repeatedly. With a sledgehammer. And a baseball bat. A metal one. Or did a wood one hurt more?

"You're rambling," she said. "We always did get carried away." The girl chuckled, and I finally pulled my attention away from her sexy body and focused on her words.

"We?" I quirked an eyebrow reproachfully, unable to stop my gaze from skating over the petite figure. She really did look like me, but there was something different in her eyes. A sort of glacial coldness and loneliness that had long since diminished since forging my relationship—or was it relationships?—with the guys.

Shrugging, she ventured a step forward.

"I am you. You are me."

A sudden chill swept over my body, down my spine, and into the soles of my feet. Darkness pierced the kitchen, so suddenly that I scrambled to my feet.

"Where am I?" My arms wrapped around my waist, but it did little to fight off the frigidly cold air. Was there a window open? That was the only explanation I could conjure up to explain the steep decline in temperature. My breath came out in puffs.

Smiling serenely, the other me extended a hand. "Come, I'll show you."

I remained still, indecisive. I wished that the guys were here. God, how I needed their strength. Mustering up what little courage I had, I accepted her hand. Her smooth fingers and palm caused me to jump. In the days since everything had gone to hell, my own were covered in blisters and unhealed callouses. I couldn't even remember a time when my hands were that soft.

She led me through the front doorway and into the street.

Snow drifted down, blanketing the grass and skeletal tree branches. A blighted sun hung high in the sky, hinting that it was already midday. Despite the cold air, the sight was peaceful. Tranquil. Almost beautiful.

"Where am I?" I whispered, spinning in a circle. I

extended my hands to catch the wisps of snow. It was something I used to do when I was younger, and I supposed the habit hadn't stopped with age. Mother had called me childish and told me that catching snowflakes was for babies. She seemed to have forgotten that I was only six when she first started reprimanding me.

"Do you remember this place?" the other me countered beseechingly. I tried to tamp down my irritation at being ignored, instead focusing on her words.

"Should I?"

"Think, Addie. Think."

I was such a condescending asshole at times.

Ignoring her, I focused once again on the fluffy snow, faded street signs, and white painted buildings. One in particular captured and held my attention. Foreboding dug its penetrating claws deeper into my spine.

The dilapidated house with its wraparound porch and chipped siding was familiar, almost eerily so. My face paled. I was looking at a ghost, both literally and figuratively.

Paint had long since flaked off, the white color resembling a muddy brown. Warped wood, nails protruding from the rickety staircase, beams with no support. It was a disaster just waiting to happen.

And it was also my happy place.

"I used to visit Ducky here," I whispered. I didn't know whether to be awed or stunned. Legs shaking, I took a step closer. "It was during winter vacation. He didn't have school, and there was a padlock on the gate surrounding the playground. We couldn't meet there. One day, we went exploring, and we stumbled across this abandoned house."

I stepped up onto the deck of the bungalow, being extra mindful of the loose nails.

"I'd completely forgotten about this place." Turning

towards the other me, I added, "We only stayed here for a couple weeks."

And they had been some of the best weeks of my life. It had been Ducky and I against the world. In the small house with plastered walls and deteriorating wood, I'd never felt more alive. Mansions had nothing on this place.

For those few weeks, this had felt more like home than anywhere else.

As I watched, enraptured, two figures meandered out of the surrounding forest. The young girl was wearing a hat that I knew belonged to the boy. His own brown hair, longer than hers, was intricately plaited away from his face.

Younger me and younger Ducky.

Both of our cheeks were red from the cold, but identical smiles brightened our faces. I remembered that time. A time when I was so happy, it didn't seem real. A time when I didn't feel the need to succumb to the pain that threatened to drown me.

Staring at her heart-shaped face, I couldn't help but note the three facets of my character. The golden girl, groomed by my parents to be the epitome of perfection. The innocent girl, naïve to the horrors this world had to offer and still holding on to hope that she would get a happy ending. And finally, the woman I had become. The woman desperately, probably irrationally, in love with seven men. The woman whose strength was unparalleled to the two pathetic girls before her.

For the first time in forever, I was proud of myself. There were so many trials I'd faced, so many monsters I'd fought, that at one point, might've had the power to tear me down. But I was so much stronger because of them. Better.

Elegant Adelaide released a heavy, wistful sigh.

"Do you remember being that happy?" she asked softly. Her eyes were trained on the two children now entering the desolate house. Ducky held young Addie's hand as if it were his lifeline.

Had he known how much I depended on him? He was wrong when he called me the sun. I wasn't. Not really. I was a darkness tarnishing everything in my path, but I relied on his light almost religiously. With him, I shone.

And damn if I didn't sound like a cliché.

Compelled by an undefinable force, I followed Ducky and younger Addie into the house, ignoring the other me's question as she had mine.

The inside was just as bad, if not worse, than the outside. The walls appeared to have crumbled years ago, cobwebs now decorating the banister and corners. Mildew and mold had corroded away what little remained of the wood. Floorboards, sporadically placed beneath my feet, were rotten. In some spots, they had completely deteriorated with age. The stench of stale water from leaking pipes and years-old mold assaulted my senses.

All in all, it wasn't the safest place for two ten-year-old kids to venture into, but it was all we had. All *they* had.

Surprisingly, or perhaps unsurprisingly, I struggled to identify with the little girl currently skipping towards the dusty couch. I couldn't find it within me to connect my historical identity with my current one. We were two separate individuals.

That girl wasn't aware of the darkness she carried. The darkness she craved.

In time, she would figure it out. It would take unbearable loss and helplessness before she recognized the seductive pulls of darkness, but she would. Of that, I was certain.

"You sure you're okay?" Ducky asked, kneeling beside her. My nose scrunched in disgust as I noticed the grit and other unsavory substances staining his knees.

Younger Addie began to tremble, eyes downcast. Her palpable fear polluted my lungs.

"No," she admitted, resigned. She glanced up at him from beneath her fringe of dark lashes. "I just don't understand why they hate me. Aren't parents supposed to love their children?"

I remembered this moment somewhat vividly. It was only hours after DOD had slapped me. Compared to some of the other beatings I'd taken and endured with a smile, this one was tame. Unfortunately, it left a nasty bruise on my cheek in the shape of a hand. Ducky had noticed it almost immediately.

Of course, he hadn't known, or even suspected, the extent of the abuse. I instead made it sound as if it were a one-time thing. A drunken fit. After arguing with him profusely, he'd agreed not to tell anyone. Hell, if I remembered correctly, we'd even made a blood bond for secrecy. Nothing was more sacred than the blood bond between two ten-year-olds.

"I understand," Ducky snorted in response to younger Addie. "My own parents hate me."

"Rick and Matilda?" I'd met his parents once before, and they seemed to adore Ducky. Showering him with affection. Baking cookies for him after school like the stereotypical suburban white mom. Watching football games on the couch. I'd been immensely jealous when I saw the bond between the three of them.

Younger Addie had a similarly perplexed expression on her face.

"No, not my adoptive parents. My birth ones," Ducky amended, and younger Addie leaned forward eagerly. It was very rare for him to talk about his life before he was adopted, and she eagerly grasped onto every fragmented piece he offered up about his past.

Though I already knew what he was going to say, I still

leaned forward as well. Only Bitch Me didn't react, her expression impassive.

"My dad beat me all the time. Beat my mom. Killed my sister." He spoke without any inflection. Facts. I knew it was a mechanism he'd adopted long ago in order to survive. Conceal your emotions. Put on a front.

God, I'd completely forgotten about that. About him. About this moment. About this life-altering confession he'd so carelessly admitted.

It was the one and only time he'd ever mentioned it. Conversation steered away from depressing topics about abusive parents and into more fun territory. Namely, a cat younger Addie wanted to adopt.

Was I really so self-absorbed that I'd repressed this memory? This confession? Was it because I didn't want to deal with his pain along with my own? I couldn't answer that question, nor did I necessarily want to. All I knew for certain was that the memory hit me like a stack of bricks.

"Why are you showing me this?" I gasped, turning away from younger Addie and Ducky. The memory was almost too painful to witness.

Bitch Me—BM—shrugged. Or BM could stand for Bowel Movements. Either name was fitting.

"He was strong without your help, and he will continue to be strong. They all will. It's not like you've been the best friend or the best girlfriend." Her lips contorted into a sneer, though I couldn't tell if it was directed at me or herself. Or us. Damn. This was really beginning to confuse me.

"Why are you saying that?"

"Because I want you to understand that they will be fine without you. It may hurt for a little bit, like a pesky bee sting, but they will survive. So now you need to decide, for yourself, whether or not you want to stay or go."

Her words held a vague coherence. Memories, slightly

blurred, pounded against my mind, demanding to be let free. There was something I had to remember, something important. Once I could recall that, I would better be able to understand the proposition BM was giving me. However, the memory faded like words etched into the shoreline. A wave would always come and eat them away.

I latched mechanically onto one of the last things she'd said instead of focusing on all of the unknowns.

"Y-You're wrong," I stuttered out. A breeze from one of the many broken windows sent goosebumps up and down my arms. I wrapped them around myself, both for warmth and comfort.

BM cocked her head to the side.

"I'm wrong? How am I wrong?"

"Declan will die." When she merely blinked rapidly at me, I hurried to explain. "He's allergic to bees. So if stung, he'll die."

CHAPTER 17

TAMSON

*O*nce the rain ceased, the sky became blood red.

Blood—a fitting similarity. The sky had opened up, released its deluge of tears, and left behind a blotchy, red-stained face. It was as if the earth was mocking me, mocking us. A physical manifestation of our own inner chaos. Turmoil. Pain. Agitation. The words were endless.

Words usually came easily to me. A product, I was sure, of the life I'd been thrown into. I once had to charm and seduce a rich heiress for a mission. Another time, I had to negotiate a hostage situation. Sarge once joked that eloquence was my middle name, but words weren't capable of mending Addie's flesh back together. No, for the first time in forever, words had failed me. No condolences, no placating sympathies, could save her life.

I cradled my head in my hands, tears that I would never shed burning behind my eyes. Like the rain, they wanted to release their torment onto the world. Also like the rain, the tears could be fatal. Not could. *Would.* If I started, I would never stop.

Sitting in the hallway outside Adelaide's bedroom door, I heard Doc's muffled voice as he said something to Sarge. Only our team leader had been allowed inside the room, overseeing the doctor's treatment of the girl we all loved.

Doc had incentive to treat her—if she died, he died. We died.

Everyone would fucking die.

Calax paced in front of me, his agitation and restlessness indisputable. The man was five seconds away from losing his mind. His entire body displayed his tension. The muscles flexed, the clenched jaw, the narrowed eyes, the hands curled into fists. He was terrifying—a beast in desperate need of a kiss from his beauty.

But a fucking kiss wouldn't be enough to wake her.

My team had always told me I was too pessimistic, too cynical. I wished I could refute their claim, but my mind kept replaying the moment the bullet speared her stomach. Despondent whimpers had escaped her blood caked lips, the sound threatening to haunt me until the day I died.

It should've been me.

That was the prominent thought battling for dominance in my head. It drowned out all others, even my fear and heartache.

Guilt.

Shame.

Love.

It should've been me.

It was no wonder she hadn't picked me—I hadn't even been able to protect her. She had relied on me, and I'd failed her. Like I'd failed my grandma.

I was such a fuck up. Like a parasite, I latched helplessly onto the only living, breathing entity in my life. My damn heart had claimed her as my own, completely ignoring the logical rebuttal from my brain that reminded me, repeatedly, of all of the reasons why she couldn't be mine. Did my heart listen? No.

And her last moments with me...

I'd been a monster. When she woke up—and despite my pessimistic nature, I'd be damned if she didn't—she would hate me for the way I treated her.

If she woke up...

My stomach clenched and tightened, threatening to expel the contents of my breakfast. How could everything change so suddenly? So drastically? So badly? Just yesterday, she'd been laughing over something Ronan said and baking with Asher. She'd been curled up with Ryder on the sofa in a whispered conversation and in Calax's embrace. She'd been teasing Sarge and practicing her sign language with Declan. She'd been putting a tentative hand through my own unruly red-brown curls, commenting on how soft they looked.

It was almost comical how quickly things could change.

Calax spun to face me abruptly, face pale and eyes wild. Unhinged. Despite his appearance, his gruff voice was uncharacteristically soft.

"I can't lose her."

I knew what he wanted.

He wanted me to tell him that everything was going to be okay, that she was going to open her eyes and smile up at him. But I couldn't. My own thoughts were running pervasive within my head, unattended, and I couldn't reel them back in. Instead of answering him, I stared stoutly ahead.

He couldn't lose her. I couldn't lose her. Fallon couldn't lose her. None of us could fucking lose her. The reality was, we *would* lose her. Unless Doc was some sort of miracle worker.

Why wasn't she fighting for us?

Why wasn't she fighting to come home?

I'd seen the fight drain from her eyes. She'd given up, both body and mind. For the briefest moment, I felt a stab of blistering anger. It burned a hole through my chest, like a branding rod. Just as quickly, the anger diminished to be replaced by something colder. She gave up because she didn't have faith that we would save her. She gave up because she didn't trust us.

Because of me.

Because I'd failed her.

Asher appeared from around the corner, a large duffle bag slung over his shoulder. Fallon had instructed him to go to the local hospital and gather all of the supplies he could as quickly as he could. Kill anyone who tried to stop him.

From the fresh blood darkening his blond hair, I concluded that he'd obeyed Fallon's orders.

"Grabbed random shit. Didn't know what I needed," he muttered. His eyes were in a perpetual daze. Ever since Adelaide had been shot, he appeared as if he was drifting through life. He couldn't even bring himself to put on his usual friendly, boy-next-door mask. No, in its place was a stone-cold killer. A hunter. An assassin.

Without a word, he pushed open the bedroom door, slipped inside, and shut it softly. I found that I couldn't bring myself to look up during that brief moment the door was open. I didn't want to see Adelaide lying pathetically in the bed, her brown curls damp with sweat, blood cascading from the gunshot wound in her stomach. Blood. So much blood.

I'd never considered myself queasy before. My job wouldn't allow me to be. But just then, I thought that I would vomit all over the carpeting.

I didn't know if I wanted to be sick or stab someone. Anyone.

Elena—the bitch—was lucky she'd left when she did. If

we had come back to see her and her traitorous team, there was no telling what we would've done. People like her made me sick to my stomach. I couldn't believe that I'd once kissed that creature—a creature who believed it was acceptable to knock the crown off another woman's head.

I knew Addie, once she woke up, would be devastated by the turn of events. She'd considered Samantha and Lilly friends, if a bit too quickly in my opinion. Even Elena had wormed her way into Addie's heart. To know that they'd betrayed her, left her for dead? That wasn't something she could easily recover from.

Declan poked his head out of the room he was wallowing in, the damn black kitten held tightly in his arms. He seemed to have this misconstrued mentality that if he held the cat as close to himself as he could, it would somehow rouse Addie from her fatal slumber.

He raised an eyebrow at me, eloquently asking for any updates. In answer, I merely shook my head. I didn't have the energy to raise my hands to sign to him, nor did I even want to talk. My body felt weak and sluggish, a physical extension of my mind.

The front door opened and closed once again, and my body automatically tensed.

"Honey, I'm home!" Ryder called cheerfully. There was a sound of flesh hitting flesh, no doubt Ronan slapping his brother, and then a slew of curses, quickly muffled.

"What the fuck are you going to do with the body?" asked Tommy indignantly. My curiosity instantly piqued at that. Body? Where the fuck had they gotten a body?

My question was quickly answered when Ryder and Ronan came around the corner. Over Ronan's shoulder was an unfamiliar male with a shock of dark hair and pasty skin.

"Where's Fallon?" Ronan asked, hoisting said body

further up when it began to slip. "I need to figure out what to do with this heavy asshole."

Tommy appeared from behind him. His sparkly pink glasses were noticeably absent from his pudgy face. He took one look at Declan, petting the squirming black cat, and then lifted his gaze to meet Calax's. Understanding dawned on his face, followed quickly by a shattering. That was the only word I could think to describe it. His entire expression *shattered*, as if he'd had his world turned upside down. As if a rock were thrown at a mirror. A pebble tossed into a once tranquil pool. He may not have loved her the way we did, but he considered her family. I didn't know which type of love was more dangerous.

Without his usual sly remark, he turned on his heel and stomped away.

Ryder and Ronan were slower to catch on, both of them engrossed with the body. Ryder was poking the man's cheek, attempting to stir him awake, while Ronan was bitching about the weight breaking his shoulders.

"Where's Addie?" Ryder asked, finally diverting his attention. His umber eyes, a strange golden color that seemed to flash yellow in the artificial lighting, widened. Before I could answer, he was already shaking his head in denial.

Ronan dropped the body unceremoniously, and it fell to the floor in an undignified heap.

"No," he whispered meekly. His attention was fixed on the closed door as if his eyes were somehow able to penetrate the wooden barrier and see the girl within. I didn't know how he knew she was in there. Sixth sense? A magnetic pull?

Before I could stop them—not that I wanted to—Ryder and Ronan shouldered their way inside. Once again, the door clunked ominously as it closed. It seemed to be an accurate metaphor.

The door closing.

Adelaide dying.

They were one and the same.

I resumed my customary position against the wall, knees pulled up to my chest and arms wrapped around both my legs. The position did little to hold myself together. My body was in shambles, but my soul had fallen to shreds the second the gun had gone off.

We weren't normal men, though.

We were hunters. Monsters. Dangerous individuals. If we were to lose our humanity, our reason for living, the entire world would pay.

There would be no survivors.

∿

DECLAN

I couldn't just stand by and watch the woman I loved fade away. I wouldn't.

As the sun dipped beneath the boughs of trees and the sky turned a metallic violet, I hoisted my bag further over my shoulder. It held an assortment of supplies we had gathered —maps, canned food, and water bottles.

Nobody noticed when I slipped outside and made a beeline towards the truck. Paint was chipped away, both from the rain and from vandalism I suspected. Rust was beginning to form around the tires, a russet brown that contrasted greatly with the midnight black exterior. The corroding death trap wasn't an ideal form of transportation, but it was all we had. The van was in worse shape.

Nobody noticed when I stared once more at the house. It was dark. Only one room had candle flames flickering intermittently behind the closed blinds. I knew that an angel would be lying on the bed in there, fighting for her life.

Nobody noticed me leave.

Nobody, that was, except for Sarge.

By the time I slid into the driver's seat and started the car, he'd slipped into the passenger side. I jumped, startled, at seeing his shadowed profile.

Fuming with an almost incandescent fury, I reached up to switch on the car light. It illuminated the dark, heavy bags beneath his eyes and the white pallor of his normally tanned skin. His hair was wildly disheveled, slipping free of its usually immaculate ponytail. To be honest, the man looked as if he was inches away from death. He looked as if he should've been the one fighting for his life, not Addie.

The thought, once again, caused my hands to clench around the steering wheel, the veins bulging. Reluctantly, I wrenched them free and turned to face Fallon fully.

"What are you doing here?" I signed.

He gave me an exasperated look. It was the look I often received when I was a child, he'd first taken me under his wing.

"What are you doing here?" he countered, his hands moving rapidly in agitation.

I saw no point in lying to him. After all, he was perceptive enough to know I was leaving in the first place. I'd once joked he had eyes in the back of his head, but that was wrong. The man had eyes *everywhere.*

"I'm leaving." Shrugging, I reached into my pocket and grabbed a yellow slip of paper. Written in delicate script that we both knew belonged to Addie was an address—Nikolai's address.

Her brother.

Fallon's eyes narrowed into thin slits as he read what we'd all already memorized. According to the maps, it was just south of downtown Atlanta. Addie described the house as a tiny bungalow style more than a farmhouse. Thirty or so minutes away from the city.

I couldn't save Addie, but maybe, just maybe, I could save her brother.

"You're going after him," Sarge signed, and even I could see that it wasn't a question. He knew my intentions, but his apathetic front gave nothing away.

Instead of answering, I settled for a nod.

"Alone." Again, I knew instinctively that it wasn't a question. This time, I didn't humor him with a response, but instead leveled him with my best glare. Was he going to stop me?

There were many reasons I had to go to Atlanta.

Nik was one of those reasons. The other?

My father.

Sarge must've seen the resolution on my face, as his body sagged in defeat. His fingers tapped against the center console, hinting at whatever lurked beneath his seemingly impassive exterior. After a moment, he nodded and tugged his seatbelt on.

I was too stunned to do anything but blink at him. Noticing my dumbstruck expression, Fallon signed,

"I'm coming with you."

"No," I argued. *"You need to stay with Addie. She needs you."*

At the mention of her name, his entire demeanor changed and tightened. His eyes flared violently.

"I know she needs me." He ran a hand through his hair once more. *"But she would never forgive herself if anything happened to her brother. We're going to get him and bring him back to her. She would want to see him when she wakes up."*

The way he spoke...

It had only just occurred to me that he didn't perceive a future without Adelaide in it. That scenario just wasn't plausible in his mind. I had the distinct feeling that if something were to happen, he would live the rest of his life in denial.

The unfeeling icy asshole loved her.

He loved her just as fiercely as I did. As Calax did. As we all did. He would be willing to die for her, be willing to sacrifice us for her.

There was no changing his mind once he got like this. Addie was his world, and if he needed to save her brother to feel useful, then he would. We were a team. All of us. Live or die together.

And Sarge had chosen death.

Without another word, I put the car into drive.

CHAPTER 18

ADDIE

I really hated Bitch Me.

As she smiled at me, the epitome of smug bitch, I resisted the urge to deck her upside the head. Damn. This must've been what Elena and the others felt on a daily basis. No wonder they'd left me for dead.

Okay, that was a lie.

There was no reason for the way they behaved. I firmly believed that us women had to stand up for one another and protect each other. I didn't like using degrading terms to describe women, but Elena? She was a bitch. I could say that without guilt.

I was a bitch too, so no one could argue that I was being biased.

Without another word, I stormed out of the house and back onto the street. Snowflakes continued to flutter down-wards, an ethereal combination of white and palest pink from the sun. I heard, rather than saw, BM follow me out. Almost instinctively, I turned back towards the house.

Younger Me was laughing at whatever Ducky said, her face alight with a childlike innocence and joy that had slowly corroded away with time. It was like the paint on a car—toxic influences diminished its beauty.

Inspecting their profiles through the dirty window, my mind wrenched me back to a day only a couple of weeks ago.

The pebble hitting my face pulled me from my slumber.

Bolting upright, I glanced anxiously around my room. Unsurprisingly, there was no one present, but that didn't stop unease from tightening my stomach. I'd been dreaming, though dreaming failed to accurately describe what I'd endured. A nightmare would've been a better description. I remembered the distinct taste of copper in my mouth. Blood. My blood. Or was it my parents' blood? I found that I couldn't recall. Try as I might, the dream slipped through my fingers. It was like trying to hold water for a long period of time—impossible.

There had been a shadow. A monster, perhaps.

And my men had been there...

Shaking my head to clear the remnants of my dream, I glanced once more at the pebble now lying beside me.

A pebble?

I didn't know why I thought I'd imagined that.

My confusion morphed into fear when a silhouette appeared in my bedroom. The moon highlighted a set of broad shoulders and an impressive, chiseled chest. He took a step closer, and I was able to see a shock of dark brown hair. Strong jawline. Arresting green eyes that saw into my very soul.

Quickly, I switched on my bedside lamp.

"Declan," I signed. "You scared the shit out of me."

He smiled sheepishly, the usual coldness I'd grown to attribute to Declan completely dissipating. In that moment, he looked almost boyish. Young.

"Sorry." *He chuckled, the sound sending delightful tingles straight to my core.* "I thought your window was closed. I was trying to be romantic. You know, throw rocks at the window and all."

My brain short-circuited at his use of the word 'romantic.' It conjured up images of him on one knee, a ring in his hand. A bouquet of roses.

But we'd never been a traditional couple, friends or otherwise.

Instead of rings, I got rocks hitting my face. Instead of roses, I got sly smiles and dark chuckles. His version of romantic varied considerably from my own. It was just one of the reasons why I loved him.

My brain rebelled at using such a word when describing my relationship with Declan, but then I instantly berated myself for my childish reaction. We were allowed to feel love for one another. We'd been best friends for years, and time had not lessened those feelings. There was nothing wrong with the emotion. The connotations had made it dirty. Wrong.

But society failed to realize that there were numerous types of love.

Romantic love.

Sexual love.

Familial love.

Platonic love.

Declan tapped my chin, garnering my attention. His expressive brows were furrowed.

"You okay?" *he signed, and I offered him a tentative smile. What would he think of me if he knew the direction of my thoughts? If he knew that I was thinking the dreaded "L-word," and not in a sisterly manner. No, the direction of my thoughts leaned towards the romantic-slash-sexual end of the spectrum.*

Great. Now I was thinking about sex. With Declan. In this bed.

And then I thought about Calax, my wonderful boyfriend, but instead of deterring me, I began to think about sex with both of them. Man, I had a secret kinky side. Three-ways. Four-ways. Freaking eight-ways. The sky was the limit. Correction—my vagina was the limit.

"How's your leg?" *Declan signed, nodding towards the black, heavy cast on said leg. I shrugged, unable to help noticing that Declan's eyes zeroed in on the swath of skin exposed on my stomach when my shoulders came up. My cheeks flushed.*

"It's seen better days. And worse days. And days in-between. Legs are annoying. I'm more of a fingers and penis type of girl."

He merely blinked at me, both because I'd forgotten to use sign language in my ramble and because of what I said. I silently prayed that I'd spoken too fast for him to read my lips, but when a delectable blush rose up his neck and to his cheeks, I knew that the gods weren't that generous. Damn my big mouth.

And my big, needy vagina.

All it needed now was a sign that said "Open for Business" in flashing, neon red lights.

Greedy, horny bitch.

"Let's talk about something else. I meant, sign about something else. Can you talk? I mean, I know you can, obviously. I heard you. Why don't you talk? Does your voice sound weird? Oh God, is that insensitive of me to ask? I give you permission to spank me. Damn. I have an unhealthy obsession with spankings. And whips. And chains. Hmmm...maybe it's just a phase."

Declan waved his hands vigorously in front of my face, and I paused in mid-speech. Mid-rant would be a more accurate description. Wincing, I dared a glance at him out of my peripheral vision. Instead of looking disgusted by my blurted confession, he appeared confused.

"I have no idea what you just said," *he admitted without preamble. Now my cheeks flamed for an entirely different reason.*

"Sorry," *I signed.* "I suck at this. Sometimes my thoughts run away from me, and my hands have trouble keeping up. Forgive me?"

A slow smile tilted his lips upwards. It caused delicious tingles to course through my body, as if I'd been shot by a bolt of electricity. Or a thousand bolts. Or a thousand bolts and a penis. Or a—

Down girl.

"Nothing to forgive."

The sound of a curse coming from outside made me jump. Declan's eyebrows furrowed.

"Everything okay?" *he signed, capturing and holding my attention.*

"Goddamn it. That was higher than I thought," *a familiar voice muttered.*

"Callie?" *I asked breathlessly. Declan watched my lips move, his brow quirking, before understanding flickered in his eyes. Instead of looking angry at the intrusion, or even jealous, he turned towards the newcomer expectantly.*

Calax's hands appeared first, gripping the sill, before his tall, muscular body was pulled through the window. He landed with a grunt on the ground, his dark hair disarrayed and dirt smeared on his high cheekbones.

"What are you doing here?" *I squeaked. My eyes rapidly flicked from Declan, perched on my bed, to Calax, and then to the diminutive sliver of space between me and my ex-best friend. I had to have been breaking thousands of rules here. Rule Number 212: No Guys Besides the Boyfriend are Allowed in the Bed.*

But Calax didn't seem perturbed at seeing Declan. Instead, he merely clapped him on the shoulder and came to sit beside me on the opposite side of the bed.

"You need to get some sleep," *he said, a hand coming up to tenderly brush a strand of hair behind my ear. I gaped at him, glanced anxiously at Declan, and then went back to gaping. Frankly, I resembled a lunatic fish forced out of water. Definitely not a sexy look on me.*

Calax smiled smugly, but ignored my inquiring gaze.

"Get some rest, baby girl. We'll be here with you until you wake up."

When I just continued to stare at him as if he had a few screws loose, Declan pulled back the blanket and slid in beside me. Calax hastily did the same on my other side.

I found myself sandwiched between two very strong, very sexy men.

Oh god. The fantasy.

It was coming true, wasn't it?

I wasn't ready for double penetration yet. My butthole was too tight. I hadn't dared put a finger up there yet. What if I farted? What if I—

Calax's chuckle cut me off in mid-mental-rant.

"I'm thinking aloud again, aren't I?" I whispered against his broad chest. I could feel the heat emitting from Declan's warm body behind me. Before Calax could answer, Declan's arm wrapped around my waist, and his legs entangled with mine. It was such an intimate embrace that pinpricks of desire radiated throughout my body. I glanced at Calax, gauging his reaction, only to find his eyes on me, the heat in his gaze lighting a path.

"You were," he admitted. Before I could react, he brought his lips to my ear.

"And when I take you from behind, you'll be prepared."

Before I could reply—because really, what could I even say to something like that? —his teeth clamped down on my sensitive lobe. An instinctive moan of pleasure, of bliss, filled the air. Calax chuckled darkly.

"Goodnight, my love."

"Goodnight," I whispered breathlessly.

Held in the embrace of two men, I drifted off to sleep. Honestly? It was the best night of sleep I had in years.

"Are you just going to stand there with a dopey expression on your face?" Bowel Movements asked snidely, snapping me out of my reverie. I glared at the little bitch, wishing that I could punch her face...and then I realized that I was actually wishing to punch my own face.

Shit got confusing.

"I was thinking," I snapped. BM gave me an exaggerated eye roll.

"Wow. That's fascinating. You must be so proud of yourself."

Had I really been that condescending?

Had I really been that much of a bitch?

Yes. Yes I had.

Turning away from BM, I began to walk down the snow-covered street. The carcasses of tree branches grazed my face as I stepped off the path and into the forest the children had emerged from.

"Where are you going?" There was more disdain than actual curiosity in her voice.

"Away," I retorted back. Twigs snapped beneath my feet, the sound loud in the unaccustomed silence. I realized, somewhat vaguely, that the lack of sound was disturbing and unnerving. There should've been critters scampering to and fro. Leaves rustling in the cold winter breeze. Birds cawing from up above. Instead, I was met with a silence that slithered over my skin like a dark, sticky tar. I rubbed at my arms instinctively, as if that gesture could somehow fight the chill that had nothing to do with the cold.

"You can't run away from this!" BM called after me. I didn't even have to look to know that she would've been rolling her eyes. Knowing her—knowing *me*, her hip would've been cocked to the side with a hand on said hip. It was a standard pose I'd perfected when I was younger. The eloquent gesture communicated how many shits I gave. Namely, none.

"I'm not technically running!" I called back, very nearly tripping over a tree branch. I would like to give credit to my ninja-like reflexes for keeping me on my feet. My training with Fallon had most definitely paid off. "I'm walking."

"You always do this." Her voice came from just above my shoulder, and I flinched. Though her tone could almost be described as dispassionate, there was a certain coldness that thickened the air. Goosebumps erupted on my flesh.

"Do what?" I asked, though I didn't care. At this point, I wanted to get as far away from her as possible.

As far away from me as possible.

I was beginning to associate BM with the girl that I hated. The girl that I used to be. Weak and selfish and with this constant pressure to be perfect and to have the world behave perfectly as well. I knew that the weight on her shoulders was suffocating. I knew, because I felt the same way even now. This was a version of myself that hadn't survived such a drowning. She was still tumbling through wave after wave, unable to find that pocket of fresh air. Her features were hardened because of what she'd been through—no love, no companionship, no guys. A slave to our parents.

Briefly, I felt pity for her.

For me.

For the girl I used to be.

I remembered that existence. It had been...lonely. There was no other word to describe it. The loneliness was like a clamp on my heart, squeezing the life from me. I'd been dying ever so painfully, and I hadn't even noticed.

"You run away from your problems," Bitch Me was saying now, and any pity I felt for her instantly diminished. I spun on my heel so quickly that she staggered back a step. Despite being the exact same height, I felt as if I was towering over. With an imperious set to my chin, I spoke through gritted teeth.

"I don't run away from my problems. Not anymore. *You* do. And I'm not you. I changed...I'm better than I used to be."

I gave her a once-over, my lips curling in disgust. I really had been a pathetic creature. Needy and undeserving of love. There were so many people I'd hurt, Ducky and Calax to name a few. My life was like a wrecking ball. Everyone in my path had paid the price, sometimes with their lives. "I'm better than you."

I had to give BM credit—she didn't cower away as I thought she would. Instead, she raised her chin and met my stare defiantly.

"You can say all you want, but I know the truth. You have feelings for all of them, don't you? All seven of them?" Something must've flickered in my face, guilt most likely, for she threw back her head in laughter. "Don't you think it would be easier to let them go? To stop stringing them along?"

Before she'd even finished speaking, I was already shaking my head.

"I'm not. Stringing them along, that is. I'm only with Calax and Ryder."

Bitch Me put a hand on her hip and tilted her head to the side. Brown tresses glowed in the waning sunlight, highlighting the strands of orange and gold. Damn, I was a hot piece of ass.

Not the time, Adelaide.

"Two boyfriends?" she said dryly. "And you believe that you're *not* stringing them along? That's low, even for you."

I didn't have to stand there and take her shit.

I knew what we had was unconventional, but it worked for us. I loved them, all of them, and they loved me. So what if it wasn't the traditional boy and girl romance? As I stated before, nothing about us was traditional. We were seven enigmas, seven tortured souls. We'd found each other when we had no one else, and faith intertwined our lives together.

There was no doubt in my mind that we belonged together.

All of us.

The realization sent me staggering back a step. I hadn't just included Calax and Ryder in that clump of people. I'd thought of all of them—all seven of them.

And me.

God, how had I been so stupid? It was so obvious that I wanted to scream.

I was in love with them. With Calax and Ryder. With Ronan, my sarcastic and sexy leprechaun. With Asher and Tamson, two of the sweetest boys I'd ever met. With the brooding Fallon. With my best friend, Declan.

BM smiled, no doubt coming to the same conclusion I had.

"You're only hurting them. If you loved them, you'd let them go."

Intuitively, I glanced over my shoulder. Seven distinct silhouettes stood in the forest. I didn't have to see any features to know who they were. The seven men who had captured my heart. The seven men who held that organ in their hands. The seven men who had the capacity to either build me up...or completely destroy me.

And I, them.

After all, love was a two-way street.

"Let them go," I parroted mechanically. My eyes slid back towards BM. With a soft smile, the first sincere smile I'd seen on her face since I met her in this shithole, she extended a hand.

"Come," she said softly. "End their pain. End your own pain. You'll be happier with me."

Indecision warred within me. I could hear the guys beckoning me to come with them. To allow them to love me. For me to love them in return.

But was that fair to them? There was only one of me and seven of them.

I wanted to run to them. Calax would hold me in his arms, offering words of comfort. Ronan would make a quip, and Ryder would respond with a sexual innuendo. Asher would berate both of them for their inappropriate behavior while smiling sheepishly down at me. Tamson would blush at the exchange, but a small smile, a smile reserved only for me, would grace his features. Declan would roll his eyes to the heavens. It was something he always did when he was searching for patience. And Fallon? He would glare at everyone present.

Except for me.

No, when his eyes met mine, they would flare with heat and something warmer. Something that I'd never seen on our fearless leader's face before. It would soften his features considerably, until the brooding male was almost entirely unrecognizable.

"This is for the best," BM assured me, no doubt privy to my inner turmoil.

"For the best," I repeated numbly. Her hand was extended towards me, tempting me, begging me to take it.

The guys were still behind me, calling for me. They wanted me to come home.

After a moment, I put my hand in hers.

CHAPTER 19

CALAX

She looked beautiful, even like that. Even with her face ashen and blood coating her skin. Even with death looming ominously over her body, threatening to take hold. I held her cold hand in my own and gently reached over to touch her cheek.

"Why isn't she waking up, Doc?" I asked, my voice unwillingly cracking. I would've liked to blame it on the lack of use the last two days, but that would've been a blatant lie. My emotions were running rampant within me. With no outlet, I had to settle for curling in on myself mentally like old, brittle paper.

Adelaide was injured, maybe even dying.

Declan and Fallon had left us with only a vague note promising that they would return.

The rest of us? We were barely holding ourselves together. Without our leader, Fallon, and our glue, Adelaide, we were lost puppies.

And then there was Tommy.

He'd locked himself in one of the spare bedrooms and hadn't come out. I wasn't even sure if he was eating, though Asher left a plate by his door every morning and night.

In a span of hours, the once modest bedroom had been entirely redesigned until it resembled a hospital room. An IV, a table full of scalpels and stethoscopes, adhesive bandages, and various painkillers, all courtesy of Asher.

I knew he and Ryder were attempting to get the generator up and running again, but the effort was futile. The thing was shot to hell and back. No amount of praying would fix the damn thing. Instead, we had to rely on the flickering glow from the sparse and unreliable candlelight. Lining the window sill. On the bedside table. Near the foot of the bed. It was a miracle that Doc was able to operate in the first place, what with his limited supplies and the scarce lighting provided.

The man looked tired. Weary. He hadn't left her bedside since this first began. Granted, we didn't really leave him much of a choice. A gun to the head was the only incentive he needed.

Addie would be horrified.

"I did all I could do," Doc responded. He leaned forward, resting his elbows on his knees and placing his head in his hands. Dark, prominent bags were evident beneath his hazel eyes. "Now it's up to her."

"What do you mean it's up to her?" I asked scathingly. Doc glanced up at me as if I were an imbecile. I just barely resisted snapping his thin neck.

We needed him alive.

For now.

After Addie recovered…

Well…

It would be in his best interest not to piss me off too much.

"She has to want to fight," he explained. "It's in her hands now."

"She's going to fight." There was no doubt in my mind of that. That was one of the things that I loved about her. And one of the things that annoyed the ever-loving shit out of me.

Doc startled at the conviction in my voice, his eyes flickering towards Addie's pale frame. I bristled at the disbelief in his expression. He didn't know her like I did. He didn't know that she would do anything for the people she loved, including fighting and winning against death itself.

"You should go get some food. And maybe find something to wash yourself off with." His nose wrinkled in distaste at the latter statement. "I'll tell you if anything changes."

I hesitated, gripping Addie's hand even tighter. I hadn't eaten in days, despite Asher's repeated attempts at getting food into me, and I hadn't washed myself off since...well...I couldn't remember when. My body was coated in a layer of blood, Addie's blood.

"You can send one of the others in here," Doc said beseechingly. "She'll be fine for the ten minutes you're gone."

Scrubbing a large hand down my face, I nodded in agreement. I was no use to Addie dead or weakened.

Without taking my eyes from the doctor, I stood and pushed open the bedroom door. Tamson sat in the entryway, eyes haunted as he stared at a blood stain darkening the carpeting. He only glanced up when I cleared my throat, eyes purposely avoiding the room—and consequently, the girl—behind me.

"I'll be back in a few minutes. Keep an eye on her?"

He hesitated, indecision disfiguring his features. I clenched my hands into fists and tucked them beneath my armpits. It was either that or punch him in the head.

"I know you don't want to see her like that. I don't want to fucking see her like that, but someone has to stay with her." Narrowing my eyes, I nodded towards where Doc was watching our exchange with rapt attention. "Unless you want her to be alone with Doc."

At those words, his resolve strengthened, and he scrambled to his feet. Doc muttered something about "taking offense to that" behind me. Without another word, Tamson strode past me and slammed the door shut.

I winced at the sound.

Alone for the first time I could remember, I wandered aimlessly into the bathroom. Since the acid rain fiasco, we hadn't been able to use the stream to clean ourselves up. Instead, Asher had brought numerous packages of water bottles. I didn't like wasting such a precious resource, but the blood staining my hands felt just as acidic as the rain. I needed it off of me.

My tired eyes took stock of my reflection in the mirror.

Blood coated my black shirt and pasty skin. It had even found its way into my dark hair. I looked as if I had been through a war zone. How was I still standing?

How was I still breathing?

I was a soldier out on a battlefield with no purpose. No leader. No reason for fighting.

Sarge had abandoned us in our time of need. The man with all the answers, all the strength, had run with only a vague note explaining why and that he had a radio with him for quick contact.

Declan, my brother, had left us.

Everyone was fucking leaving us. Leaving me.

With more vigor than I intended, I pulled off the cap of a water bottle and dumped it on my head. The water was warm from being inside for so long, and it did little to lessen the blood on my skin. Instead, it merely turned the color pink. For some reason, I found that hysterical.

Fucking pink blood.

Addie would have a field day with that.

I conjured up images of her perfect, heart-shaped face. That fire in her eyes I'd come to both fear and love. The brown tresses that were just as soft as they appeared. The tenderness in her face when she told me that she loved me. *Me*. A beast. A monster.

My laughter contorted into heart-wrenching sobs. I gripped the sink until my knuckles turned white.

I couldn't lose her.

Not again.

I'd thought I had lost her once, and that pain had been unbearable. Now, I knew that she loved me. I knew what it felt like to be with her, to be loved by her, to taste her. She was a drug, and I was an addict.

Losing her would be the death of me. I wouldn't be able to survive such a fatal wound.

I'd lost everything and everyone in my life. I couldn't lose her as well.

My body sank to the ground, my legs unable to support my weight.

For the first time I could remember, I cried.

I cried for the little boy who'd lost his innocence. I cried for the family I never had. I cried for the girl I loved and lost.

It didn't completely diminish the pain I felt.

But it helped.

RYDER

"They'll be fine," Asher said easily, the katana sword cleanly slicing through flesh and bone. The Rager fell at his feet, a collection of sinewy, pale skin and black veins. He offered me a timid smile while simultaneously wiping the blood off on his jeans.

The blood of Ragers was not like normal blood. It wasn't red like you would expect, but instead a strange black color like molten onyx stone. It was as thick as tar and smelled something fierce.

"I don't want to talk about it," I mumbled, tossing a dagger into a Rager that was running towards Asher. The creature dropped like a bag of rocks, the copper handle protruding from its scalp.

"You do this a lot," Asher pointed out. He swung his sword in a swooping arc, effectively beheading three more Ragers.

"Do what?"

There was a reason I'd joined Asher on this supply run, and it wasn't to talk about my fucking feelings. No, I'd already decided I would keep them buried away. No amount of digging could uncover them.

The pharmacy we'd chosen to raid was a small mom-and-pop shop just at the edge of town. Since it wasn't a brand name, the building had been left alone during the initial riots and panic. The shelves were still lined with unopened medicine bottles and cans of food. The pungent aroma of stale milk and weeks old meat assaulted my senses.

I didn't know how the Ragers had gotten into this building, which had been padlocked shut. Perhaps they'd been in there when the virus initially hit. Perhaps they'd thought this building was a sanctuary—food, medicine, water, shelter. The essentials needed to live. To survive.

To flourish.

And now look at them—brainless monsters getting slaughtered.

There was a sort of sick, dramatic irony in that. My twisted mind wanted to laugh at the poetic justice.

Once the last Rager was taken care of, Asher turned towards me. The disgusting, black blood was plastered on his cheeks, staining his blond hair.

"Addie is going to be—"

"Don't you dare say fine!" I snapped, pointing a quivering finger at him. "Don't you dare fucking say it."

That was the last thing I wanted to hear—a false fucking promise. My insides convulsed, a strange combination of fear and an incandescent fury. I didn't need Asher to lie to me about something like that. No, we both knew that she wasn't fine. She was anything *but* fine.

And I wasn't man enough to be there with her.

For her.

She was dying, and I'd left her like a coward. I'd been self-ish, unable to see her lying immobile on that bed. She'd once been such a vibrant flame, full of life, that it physically pained me to see her like that. My heart rebelled at the idea of losing her. The damn organ wouldn't listen to my logical brain. It held onto hope—that dreaded, evil emotion.

Hope was stupid. We built up these walls, these impene-trable fortresses made entirely of our mangled faith and hope. When hope faded, though, we were left with nothing but walls. These walls couldn't be broken.

So no, I didn't believe in holding onto hope.

Hope was for dumbasses.

The sooner I could accept the inevitable, the happier I would be.

But damn if my heart didn't pound against my ribcage,

demanding me to stay strong. Adelaide was going to live. She had to, for my own sanity.

Without another word to Asher, who was regarding me warily as if I were a snake preparing to strike, I began to shove miscellaneous items into my bag. The monotonous movement allowed me to believe, if only for a second, that my life wasn't completely falling to shambles. That I hadn't only lost the girl I loved, but two of my brothers. For that brief moment, as sun slashed through the surprisingly clean window, I could pretend.

It was like being on stage. I was a performer, through and through. This was just another performance.

Asher, mercifully, changed the subject.

"There's a lot of them," he mused, indicating the Ragers. I grunted in response. "More and more." He paused, staring down at a decapitated body. I wouldn't have been able to tell you the gender. It could've been a female with a larger frame, or it could've been a male. It was disconcerting to see a body disconnected from its head.

I swallowed the bile that threatened to explode out of me.

"What measures do you think we can take to prevent it?" he asked, nudging the monster with his foot. "The infection spreading, I mean."

"I don't fucking care."

And I didn't. It no longer mattered to me if I lived or died. Became infected.

There was no point to any of it anymore.

Asher gave me a long look, no doubt questioning the sincerity of such an answer, before he sighed heavily. It was a resigned sigh. I wasn't sure if he agreed with my statement or just accepted it.

Silence thickening the air until it was almost palpable, we worked at loading the van. Like the rest of the vehicles, the acid rain had caused the exterior to rust and corrode away.

Ragers, faces hideously disfigured from the rain, roamed the street. Fortunately, they didn't pay us any mind, instead focusing on attacking one another.

Asher was right—these monsters were scary, but not in the traditional sense. There was no logical explanation as to why some people had been turned while others remained human. What attracted the worms to certain individuals? I was unsure if this question would ever be answered besides in vague theories and unconfirmed explanations.

"I love her too," Asher said, his voice breaking through the silence like the slash of a keen knife. I startled at his words, despite the fact that I'd already suspected as much. Before I could stop myself, I snorted. The sound was unintentionally malicious. I wasn't purposely trying to be a dick. Honestly. I was strung too tight, and it was only a matter of time until I erupted like a fucking volcano. Instead of lava, however, I would spew blood.

"Have fun loving a dead girl."

CHAPTER 20

DECLAN

*W*e drove through the night, alternating sleeping in the passenger seat and driving.

It was impossible for us to talk. Sarge wasn't, by nature, a talkative person, and I had no energy to raise my hands. Instead, we sat in companionable silence. Moonlight spliced the upholstered seat, painting the car's interior in a soft, golden glow.

According to the map, we were still a few hours away from our destination. My fingers tapped against my knee as my unease strengthened and grew.

Was I making a terrible mistake by leaving Addie when she needed me? I didn't know, and I didn't want to fixate on it. Sarge expertly steered the truck down the backroads, avoiding the numerous stray cars with all of their doors thrown open and the occasional dead body. Ragers chased after us, hands curled into claws, before they quickly became distracted by one another. More than one fight broke out, a tangle of limbs and hair and blood.

So much blood.

Blood loss never seemed to deter them. If anything, it only seemed to spur them on. The grotesque sight was both mesmerizing and disgusting. I didn't know if I wanted to look away or continue watching.

The car suddenly slid to the side, balancing precariously on two wheels before skidding to a stop. I reached out, grabbing the oh shit handle. Wide-eyed, I turned to meet Sarge's gaze, but he wasn't looking at me. Instead, he was focused on something in the rearview mirror. Or someone.

I spun around with an almost blistering speed and came face to face with a familiar figure.

Chubby cheeks, tangled locks of hair, eyes currently narrowed.

Tommy.

And from the vein pulsing in Fallon's neck and his erratic movements, I figured he was bitching Tommy out. Tommy, of course, remained impassive if not slightly irritated. He crossed his arms over his chest and raised his chin defiantly. He didn't speak, but instead allowed Sarge to grill him. His face turned redder and redder the more Sarge droned on. I sort of wished I could hear what was being said. I imagined it was a lot of creative language and curse words.

Sarge turned his face towards the window, either too pissed to continue speaking or trying to restrain himself from murdering the little asshole.

I, however, kept my eyes narrowed on the little shit. He didn't cower under my penetrating gaze, but instead sat up straighter.

"Why are you here?" I signed. Tommy's eyes flickered to Sarge as he translated.

"I followed you, dumbass." The asshole exaggeratedly opened his mouth, each word overly pronounced.

"Why?"

I leveled him with a glare to stress that simple word.

"Because." He sneered at me, the expression contorting his chubby face. "I couldn't just sit there and do nothing."

"How did you know I was leaving?"

Only Sarge knew I was leaving, and that was because the bastard had eyes everywhere. But Tommy? How had he known?

Tommy rolled his eyes heavenwards. "I stalked you."

Well, okay then.

I would say I was surprised, but…

Fuming, I turned towards Sarge.

"What do you suppose we do about him?" I signed, aware that Tommy no doubt couldn't understand me and was getting annoyed. Added bonus, if I was being completely honest.

"Leave him to die," Sarge responded.

Tommy began to rapidly move his hands, a series of random gestures and dance moves. His middle finger made an appearance on more than one occasion. I rolled my eyes and ignored him. Hopefully, that irritated the little fucker.

"We can't leave him to die," I signed. Sarge blinked at me with the innocence of a wolf. When he just continued to stare at me, unperturbed, I hurried to add, *"Addie would be pissed."*

At that, he released a heavy sigh, his shoulders sagging. Once again, he'd admitted defeat in the name of Addie.

For Sarge to decide not to kill someone was real progress. Adelaide was rubbing off on him.

Tommy tapped my shoulder persistently, demanding my attention, and I reluctantly turned to face him. He smiled smugly, an imperious set to his chin.

"I know where you're going," he said. "You're going after Addie's brother, correct?"

When I didn't respond, Tommy took my non-answer as confirmation. His smile grew until it practically cut his face in half.

"Well, I want to come too. I need to do something with myself. I can't just sit around..." His eyes dropped, tears welling and cascading down his pudgy cheeks. He angrily brushed the stray tears away, the break in his brash front irritating him. With a shuddering breath, he met my gaze resolutely. "I'm coming. And there's nothing you can do about it."

Suddenly, Sarge's suggestion to leave him for dead didn't sound as bad.

Tempting, actually. Very, very tempting.

~

RONAN

She fit against my body perfectly.

Warm and soft, her body molding against mine. Lips cherry red. Eyes that never seemed to stick to one color but instead alternated between metallic violet and light blue. It all depended on where she was positioned in the sunlight. The sun was attracted to her, as it should be.

Like called to like, after all.

"What are you thinking about?" Her voice was thick with sleep. The raspy sound made my cock harden automatically.

"You," I answered softly. I tentatively brushed her hair behind her ear, allowing my fingers to linger on her flushed cheek. She was so beautiful that it physically hurt. An almost ethereal beauty. A beauty you would find in paintings, not in real life.

"Well stop thinking about me," she said with an embarrassed giggle.

How could I not think about her?

How could she not consume my every waking thought and be the star of all my dreams?

I tightened my arms around her, loving the way she felt in my embrace. I'd never believed in fate or soulmates, but my heart couldn't deny that Addie had been put on this world to complete my soul. With her, I was whole.

"I always think about you." I pressed my face against her hair, inhaling her unique scent. Peppermints almost, from the shampoo we'd stolen on our first supply run. I'd never associated that delicious scent with her before, but just then, it was all I could think about.

Who knew that peppermint could be sexy?

"Did you just sniff me?" she asked in disbelief, and I chuckled darkly.

"Yup."

"No shame."

"Nope."

I kissed the hollow of her throat, relishing her shiver of pleasure.

"I love you," I said softly. Sincerely. It was the first time I'd said those words to anyone outside of my family and brothers. I'd had dozens of girls, some of them I'd even considered as girlfriends, but none evoked such a reaction from within me. Love, for so long, was nothing but an elusive fantasy. It was something I would see in movies, hear about on television, watch couples wistfully through cafe windows. I'd never thought I would associate that word with me.

She was silent, no doubt lost in her own thoughts, before she responded.

"Why do you love me?"

The question took me by surprise. My arms loosened, and I

pulled back to look at her. She was anxiously gnawing on her lower lip, eyes flickering from her feet, to the quilt on the bed, to the drawn curtains. Anywhere but my probing gaze. I gently tilted her chin up, urging her to meet my eyes. I wanted her to see the absolute devotion I felt for her. The love. I would do anything for her. Live. Die. Dismember.

"Why wouldn't I love you?"

She tried to pull her chin away from my hand, but I refused to let her go.

"You're everything to me and my team. Funny, smart, insane." I smirked at the last word, and she rolled her eyes. "I'll never get tired of listening to your inner ramblings. Or your stupid, perverted jokes. What makes it even funnier is the fact that you don't know they're perverted. I love you because you're too pure for this world, too good for someone like me, but yet you don't see that. You don't see the flaws in a person, only the good. You don't see what a fuck up I am, what fuck ups we all are. How could I not love you?"

Her lower lip quivered, and fresh tears sprang to her eyes. When the first tear fell, I leaned forward to catch it in my mouth. She shivered delicately beneath me, and that shiver gave me the courage to rewrap my arms around her and position her securely on my lap. She nuzzled the side of my face, her warm breath stirring the hair on my neck.

"I love you too."

It was the first time she'd spoken those words aloud, and my insides tightened. Fucking butterflies fluttered, demanding release. Before I could stop myself, I tilted her head up and pressed my lips against her own. She yielded immediately, her tongue slipping out to coax my own into submission. Licks of fire ran down my spine, from my fingers to my toes. My hands tangled in her brown tresses, pulling her closer. I needed her closer as much as I needed air to breathe.

Her hands grabbed eagerly at my shirt, pulling it up so we could be skin to skin. I groaned low in my throat. With a reverence

I wasn't used to, she began to trace the dips and curves of my abs. The prominent V leading down my pants. Down and down.

Her hands were so cold, almost unhealthily so. It felt as if I was being touched by an icicle.

"Addie..." I murmured, pulling away. She needed to get warmed up. Perhaps I could start a fire...

Her face was pale, the shadows beneath her eyes pronounced. As I watched, horrified, blood dripped from her nose. Her ears. Her eyes. I screamed helplessly.

Where was Sarge?

Calax?

Ryder?

Why was I all alone?

A sob broke free as I held her dying form. Her head lolled to the side, the light leaving her eyes.

"No..." I whispered. "No. No."

"NO!"

I woke up with the word on my lips. Sweat drenched my skin and ran down my face.

Just a dream.

Just a bad fucking dream.

Gasping, I bolted upright and glanced around the darkened room. My heart was hammering, and my hands were shaking. Fear clamped my throat closed, strangling me. It had felt so real.

Her dying in my arms...

Shivers of revulsion rocked my body forward. I rubbed at the skin of my arms as if that gesture could somehow wipe away the remnants of blood from my dream. I yawned, stretching my taut muscles as sleep threatened once again to claim me.

Shouting from down the hall roused me further from my slumber. With a speed I didn't know I possessed, I jumped from my bed and hurried out of my room. I barely noticed that I was completely naked. No time for me to put on shorts.

I barreled through the door of Addie's room, fear snaking around my throat like an iron clamp.

"What's happening?" Calax was screaming when I entered. Tamson stood pale-faced by the door. Doc was standing over Adelaide, his hands on her chest as he began compressions. Her face was pale—as pale as it had been in my dream.

"No," I whispered.

Briefly, my mind flickered back to that old nursery rhyme I was told as a kid. Humpty Dumpty or whatever. But it was the equivalent to a fairy tale. It never reflected reality.

No number of horses or men…

…would put Addie back together again.

CHAPTER 21

ADDIE

I placed my hand in BM's.

Her smile was smug, predatory even, and her eyes possessed a voracious hunger, primal and carnal. I met her smile...and then roughly pulled her to the ground. She let out a gasp, and I twisted my body so I was on top of her. Jamming my elbow into the back of her neck, I hissed,

"I'm not leaving them." As an afterthought, I added, "Bitch."

She lifted her head up, lips curving into a feral sneer. I would almost describe it as a snarl.

Frankly, it was not a sexy look on me.

"So you're choosing to be selfish," she hissed. I pressed her face into the dirt, and she let out a cry.

"No," I answered evenly. "I'm choosing them. Always."

I could hear the men behind me, my men, coaxing me to come home. I would attempt to heed their call, even if it killed me.

"You bitch." Her face began to change and contort, becoming something entirely unrecognizable. Eyes turning a deep, garnet red. Teeth elongating. Nose protruding from her face. The change was so drastic, so sudden, that I staggered off of her, landing on my ass.

She towered over me, her features more monster than human.

Pain erupted on my calf as her claws dug into my skin. Hissing, I feebly kicked at the grotesque creature. I didn't even want to refer to her as BM anymore. No, there was no resemblance to the girl I once knew. I was staring into the eyes of the devil herself.

And she was furious.

"Unfortunately," she began, her voice a low growl that pulsated deep within me. It was a sound I'd never heard before, a sound that I only thought existed in movies. Goosebumps erupted on my skin that had little to do with the cold. She cracked her neck from side to side. "I can't let you leave."

Well...shit.

~

FALLON

The house was a cute bungalow style with a wraparound porch and hanging plants. A white picket fence greeted us as we drove up, further highlighting the homey feel the house was emitting. Two cars were in the driveway, the untarnished paint hinting that this area might've been spared from the acid rain. I wondered what storms they had faced. Earthquakes? Tornadoes? Floods?

"Well...this place looks fucking cozy," Tommy drawled. He pushed his head between the two seats and folded his arms on the center console. I didn't know how I hadn't noticed him before. The shit face had been unnaturally quiet where he'd sprawled himself out in the backseat. With the engine roaring and my own thoughts a mess, I hadn't even realized he was there until he'd showed himself. I really was losing my edge.

"Language," I said absently.

My entire attention was fastened on the closed window blinds. From what little I gathered, numerous houses on this street still had electricity. A small miracle, I supposed.

"Do you think anyone is home?" Declan signed.

Sighing heavily, I shrugged.

No, I didn't think anyone was home. The entire neighborhood was too silent. Too still.

Too dead.

The epitome of a ghost town. What memories haunted these streets?

Instead of saying all that, I slid out of the car and slammed the door shut. The air was warm, humidity making my shirt stick to my skin. My hair was matted to my scalp.

Mosquitos buzzed overhead, the sound deafeningly loud.

"Don't let them bite you," I warned Tommy while simultaneously signing to Declan. "We don't want to accidentally get infected."

Besides the worms and their origins, we still had no idea exactly how the virus was spread. I'd tried contacting my uncle but hadn't been able to get ahold of him. Or my father, for that matter.

Or Olivia.

I tried to make myself look as unimposing as possible, an unsurprisingly hard feat given my immense size and broad shoulders. The last thing I wanted to do was scare this family away. They didn't know me, and without Addie as a mediator, they would have trouble trusting our ragtag group.

Tommy shoved me aside and strutted towards the front

door. I watched him, my brow creasing with a frown. He was an annoying little shit, but he was growing on me. I was beginning to think of him as a younger, albeit annoying, brother. Without waiting for me, Tommy rapped his fist against the door.

Rolling my eyes, I hurried to catch up with him.

"Nobody is answering." He paused, squinting at the doorway as if he would be able to see through it. "I'm going to break in."

"You are not going to—"

Before I could finish my sentence, Tommy kicked the door down.

Kicked the fucking door down, as if he was a badass action hero instead of a tweenager. Of course, he stumbled over his own two feet, fell to the floor on top of the broken door, and began cursing up a storm. Chuckling, I helped him up and brushed plaster and dust off of his shoulders.

"Careful, there," I said. He glared at me in response, eye twitching.

Literally, twitching.

The smile left my face as a pervasive smell pummeled my senses. My eyes watered, and I immediately brought my hand to my nose in order to stunt the overwhelming scent. I'd been around enough dead bodies to know what that smell meant.

"What the fuck is that?" Tommy gasped. I was too shocked to reprimand him for his crude language. The source of the smell was soon discovered as we moved farther into the small house. The living room, consisting of two floral couches, a flat screen television, and a water stained coffee table, was splashed in blood. It was everywhere, staining the walls and carpeting and tiny cherubic statue in the corner of the room.

Two bodies were lying on the ground.

My fear dissipated, transforming into something that resembled relief, when I noted that the two figures were both older. An aging woman, brown hair streaked with gray and white, and a wrinkled faced man. The woman had been dismembered, her arms disconnected from her body and her body separated from her head, the source of the excessive amount of blood loss I imagined. The man died of a gunshot wound to his head.

In his cold hand, he held a gun.

Tommy began to sob softly, and I immediately winced at the sound. I wished that I'd shielded him from all of the horrors in this world. He was too young, too innocent, to endure such tragedies.

"Wait outside," I said gruffly, venturing a tentative step closer. A broken photograph on the coffee table captured and held my attention. Hand trembling, I picked it up and surveyed the family smiling back at me. The man and woman, the same man and woman currently lying dead on the floor, had their arms around a little boy.

Brown, tousled hair. Emerald eyes. Red headphones around his neck.

His gaze was distant, not fixated on the camera but on a spot in the far distance. He didn't look uncomfortable, merely dazed. I remembered Adelaide telling me that he had autism.

"He's not here," Tommy said. His voice was a strangled gasp.

I frowned, listening intently.

Outside, a bird chirped. The day was peaceful, serene, and a contrast to the horror that had taken place inside of this house. It almost seemed to be mocking me, mocking the dead bodies. The slanting sunlight illuminated the scene like a giant spotlight. Tremors of revulsion ran down my body.

God, this was disgusting.

This *world* was disgusting.

It was easy for me to see what had happened. The blood was semi-fresh, maybe only a few days old, but there were no Ragers present.

The woman had been attacked. The man had freaked out and had committed suicide.

And Nikolai? He was nowhere to be found.

It occurred to me that he might've been dead, but I refused to believe it. I couldn't fail Adelaide now, not when she needed me.

Not when I'd already failed her once before.

I thought through everything I'd heard about this elusive Nik.

There were only a few things I knew about him. One, he was autistic. Two, he loved music. And three…

Nothing. I didn't know anything about him.

"Nik!" I bellowed. "Adelaide sent us!"

I didn't know what I was hoping. The door to be thrown open and Nik to come hurrying out? For him to pop his head over the couch?

"Nik!"

Tommy gave me a reproachful look, shouldering me out of his way. He cupped his mouth to amplify his voice.

"Nikky boy!" Tommy called. "Your crazy ass sister sent us! You know which one? The insane girl with brown hair? Talks to herself? Ring any bells?"

There was the sound of footsteps upstairs.

"Stay here," I instructed Tommy, though I doubted he would listen. Of course the little shit immediately ran up the staircase, ignoring my curses as I hurried to keep pace. "Damnit, Tommy."

We raced down the hallway, stopping in front of an open

door to a bedroom. Spaceships on the blankets. Framed photographs on the walls. Everything was immaculately displayed, as if the owner had a keen eye for cleanliness. My eyes latched onto a small photo sticking out of the gilded edge of a mirror. The boy I recognized as Nikolai was staring down at an iPod. A young girl, maybe thirteen, had her arm wrapped around him, smiling brightly at the camera. She was so young. So innocent.

Adelaide.

Instinctively, I took the picture down and shoved it into my pocket. When Addie woke up, she would want this memory of her brother.

"Over here!" Tommy screamed, seeming to forget or ignore the fact that I was only inches away from him, and I turned towards where he was standing.

He was looming over a figure huddled in the closet. His hair was greasy, smeared with blood, and dirt streaked his hollowed face. It appeared as if he hadn't eaten in days, as his body was beginning to display malnourishment. His cheeks were sunken, and his skin was pasty.

Slowly, as to not scare him further, I crouched down to his level.

"Nikolai?" I asked softly. He was exactly as Addie described him, down to the red headphones. His eyes rested on my shoulder. "Addie sent us. Your sister sent us."

The only indication he heard me was the slightest twitch of his head. His hands twirled the black cord of his headphones, around and around his finger. They weren't plugged into anything, but I imagined he kept them on solely for comfort.

"We're not going to hurt you," I continued. Slowly, I reached into my pocket and grabbed out a beaded necklace. It was one Adelaide had worn frequently back at the resort. A gift from her father, she'd said. Nik's eyes widened in recognition. "My name is Fallon, and this is Tommy. Over here is…"

I paused, glancing around the room with narrowed eyes. "Where the fuck is Declan?"

CHAPTER 22

ADDIE

The sun broached the horizon, painting the sky an almost metallic violet. I held the rock in a tight, white-knuckled grip, panting. The winter air stirred both my hair and the skeletal branches of nearby trees.

My eyes flickered from the blood, a surprisingly dark color, staining the rock to the person at my feet.

The girl.

Me.

Or at least the old me.

I found that I couldn't muster up enough strength to care as I smashed the rock against her face. With each hit, I could feel a piece of myself breaking. Leaving. The girl's face—my face—was distorted, grotesque almost, and held no resemblance to the girl she once was. She'd been slowly chipped away, each swing of the rock making her features entirely unrecognizable.

The rock clattered to the ground, my muscles loosening

as my courage dwindled. Nothing could change what had transpired. Not the sun cresting the tree boughs. Not the birds balancing precariously on a low branch, mocking me with their silence. Not the air that seemed to get colder and colder as the seconds dragged on.

No, nothing could change what had happened. What I'd done.

The murder.

The massacre.

Darkness seeped through the edges of my vision like a black curtain being pulled closed. I could hear my guys, their voices the most beautiful sound in this god-forsaken forest, and I trudged forward.

I had to get to them.

I had to go home.

I had to.

All I could think about was BM's shattered, disbelieving expression as I'd pounded the rock into her face. There were no coherent thoughts in my head, no conscious thinking, besides the fact that I needed to return home to my guys.

Her face became even more unrecognizable with newly added bruises and bloody scabs, each hit tainting something in my soul simultaneous with the skin chipping away and the bones cracking. She wasn't the only one that had died that day.

I found that I had no regrets. I didn't like that girl, the girl I'd once been, and I was happy she was dead.

It was time to go home.

Snow flurried around me, water seeping through my thin leggings. Still, I trudged towards where my guys were silhouetted. They were calling my name, begging me to come home.

A large figure extended a hand—Calax, my rock, my protector, my best friend—and I gripped it with my own.

Darkness clouded my vision, but I kept my hand firmly in his. I wouldn't let go.

I would never let go.

~

I BLINKED, attempting to articulate where I was and how I'd gotten there. Dim light broke through the darkness I was accustomed to. The product, I was sure, of multiple candles. I was lying in a bed, blankets pooled around my feet. And I was wearing...

Only my bra?

A slightly familiar male leaned over the bed. He had dark hair, an almost dirty blond color with black streaks, and a round, cherubic face. Memories came rushing to the forefront of my mind with an almost blistering speed, assaulting me.

The store.

Elena.

Bikini.

Greg.

Gun.

Doc.

That was his name, I recalled vaguely. Not his real name, but his title. He'd been in the store...

When Greg shot me.

"How are you feeling, Addie?" His voice was calm, soothing almost.

"W-Where's Tamson?" I stuttered, attempting to sit up. "And the others?"

"They're fine. It was you that we were worried about." His eyes darkened slightly. "Do you remember what happened?"

"Do I remember that you shot me? Yes, I have a rather vivid memory of that, thank you very much."

Face twisting, he folded his arms over his chest and scowled at me.

"I didn't shoot you. I saved your life."

"After you shot me," I pointed out helpfully. Really, the man should be grateful that I wasn't castrating him. Getting shot? Ten out of ten, would not recommend.

As if summoned by the thought, pain reverberated throughout my body.

Groaning, I catalogued my injuries.

My stomach burned with a sharp pain that radiated down my spine. My body as a whole was heavy, leaden, and tired. The combination was uncomfortable but not horrible. I could survive it.

Correction—I *had* survived it.

Blinking at the hideous stitches on my stomach, I diverted my attention back towards Doc. He regarded me with a clinical detachment common in most doctors.

"How am I alive?"

Because I should've been dead. I'd felt the life draining from my body as if I were a faucet turned on. Though I was scared of what was to come, I'd accepted death.

I would've welcomed death gratefully if it kept my men alive.

Doc pursed his lips, eyes once more landing on my stomach. It would scar, of course, but it only served to remind me of all I'd conquered. Death. Pretty badass, if you asked me. And what was one more scar to the inventory?

"The bullet was a clean in-and-out," he said after a moment of silence. "Once I was able to stop the bleeding, it was up to you whether or not you were going to pull through."

"Me?"

Before he could respond, the door was pushed open. Tamson stood in the doorway, the flames from the candles highlighting his sunken skin and disheveled hair. He paused when he took stock of me, his mouth opening and closing. In his gaze, I could see a multitude of emotions.

Shock.

Relief.

Pain.

Happiness.

Love.

It was the last one that caused my throat to close and tighten with an undefinable emotion. My heart fluttered, and my stomach churned. How had I not realized it before?

Tamson loved me.

And I loved him.

It wasn't the same type of love I felt for Calax and Ryder, but I was beginning to believe love was fluid. There was no set definition for it. Love was purposefully vague, designed to conform to each person's own interpretation.

I loved Calax and Ryder and Tamson.

And Fallon, Asher, Ronan, and Declan.

I loved them all so much, I thought my heart would explode. Break. These men had the potential to break my heart, just because I loved them.

"You're okay," I whispered. I tried to sit up, but Tam raced towards my bedside and put a restraining hand on my shoulder.

"Rest." His eyes roamed over my body, no doubt analyzing every injury. They stopped once they reached the protruding, jagged mark on my stomach. A forlorn expression darkened his features, there and gone too quickly for me to comment on. That was replaced by a certain reverence, a certain tenderness, that made tears well in my eyes.

I grabbed his hand in my weak one, stunned to feel it shake and tremble beneath my grip. His whole body quivered as if he'd been shot through with electric currents. One look into his eyes, and I could see decades of grief and pain from the few days—weeks? —I'd been unconscious.

With a sudden burst of courage, I reached a hand out and gently pulled him down to my awaiting lips. I didn't care that I'd been unconscious for days and that I hadn't brushed my teeth during that time. I didn't care that I was probably a disgusting mess. No, all I cared about was the man above me. The man who'd somehow stolen and kept a piece of my heart.

It was a slow kiss, almost as if he was mapping out my lips. He met me stroke for stroke but never tried to deepen it. It was the kiss I would've expected from old lovers. A kiss that had no reason to be rushed. A kiss that promised thousands of others.

I didn't hear the door open and close until a shadow loomed over us ominously.

"You're awake," Calax said softly. I broke free from Tamson, face burning, only to see nothing but relief in the giant's face. Ryder stood behind him, a similar expression on his own.

No jealousy.

No pain.

No betrayal.

Only relief and an immense happiness that I was alive. Acceptance. Love. I knew I shouldn't have expected anything else, but the confirmation was very nearly my undoing.

Calax reached me first, eyes tracing my features as if he meant to memorize them. Tears brimmed in his eyes, but his smile was radiant.

"Don't you ever fucking do that again. I will bring you back to life just to kill you myself." He moved to kiss my lips, but I turned my face away. When his eyes flashed with hurt, I hurried to explain.

"My breath is probably rancid. I heard that the government was thinking about using it as a weapon of mass destruction against the Ragers."

Rolling his eyes, Calax gently turned my face back towards his and brushed his lips against my own. If he died, he only had himself to blame. What romance novels and movies failed to mention was morning-slash-unconscious breath. It was a real, horrid thing. Trust me.

"Kitten," Ryder said, coming to stand on the other side of the bed. Tam graciously stepped aside and moved to stand near my feet. "Don't scare me like that. I'm an old fucking man."

He, too, pressed his lips to mine, not seeming to mind or care that I'd just kissed two of his best friends. Or that, you know, I was a disgusting, greasy mess of blood and sweat.

There was only love in his gaze.

Ronan stepped up next, expression unsure and almost shy. Timid. It wasn't an emotion I was used to seeing on my eccentric leprechaun.

"I'm glad you're okay, Princess," he whispered roughly. He lowered his lips to my cheek. The chaste gesture made my stomach flutter and heart race.

God, I loved him. I loved them all.

Ronan froze, eyes widening in his handsome face. Ryder began to chuckle, a relieved albeit terse sound. Raspy almost, as if he hadn't laughed in a while. I wasn't used to a somber Ryder, and I vowed to rectify that.

Before I could refute what I'd accidentally said aloud, Ronan's lips touched mine.

A graze of lips.

There and gone before I could blink. He rested his forehead against mine, eyes promising what would come.

"I love you too."

Asher came to stand beside Calax. He didn't have to say anything, as his eyes spoke volumes. There was a story in those blue orbs, a story that hinted at pain and darkness behind his happy façade. A story that narrated the life of a man that loved a girl.

I tried to convey my own feelings with an eloquent smile. But...

There were two people missing. Where was Declan, my childhood best friend, and Fallon? A strangled sob escaped me at the realization. There was only one reason why they wouldn't be there with me, but I refused to believe it.

They couldn't be dead.

No. No. No.

"They're fine," Calax assured me, tentatively brushing at my hair. All of the guys were being extra gentle with me, extra attentive, as if I were cracked glass, one drop from being shattered. The attention was unnerving but not entirely unpleasant. "They left a note. They'll be back soon."

"And Tommy?"

Calax's eyes widened, and he whipped his head towards Ryder, who shrugged. Both of them glanced at Asher, who subtly shook his head no, and then they all turned towards Ronan and Tam. At their guilty expressions, indignation speared a hole through my chest. I was in love with a bunch of fucking assholes.

"Have you guys checked on him?" I asked, making sure to say each word slowly. All of the guys refused to make eye contact. "Where the fuck is my little psycho?!"

I tried to sit up yet again, but a sharp pain in my stomach prohibited such a movement. I hissed through gritted teeth and slowly lowered myself back down.

"About that..." Ryder trailed off at my murderous glare. "I love you?"

"Somebody go check on Tommy before I murder you all." Wincing yet again, I turned towards Doc. "And my stomach freaking hurts."

He nodded, a weary grin tilting his lips up.

"Yes, getting shot can do that to a person. You're going to be on bed rest for a couple weeks, maybe even months. I'll do everything I can to help make you comfortable."

"Thanks, Doc."

He quirked a brow. "Don't get me wrong. Greg and his buddies were sexist, kidnapping assholes, but the last thing I wanted to do was end up being the private doctor for you and your harem. If there wasn't a constant knife to my throat or gun on my back, I would've let you die." He shrugged unapologetically, and the twisted part of me appreciated his candor. The guys, however, would not appreciate such a sentiment. I turned towards them, now huddled near the doorway, to gauge their reactions towards Doc's announcement and caught a snippet of their conversation.

My eyes narrowed, and my voice sliced through the air like keen throwing knives. "What the fuck do you mean you have a prisoner?"

CHAPTER 23

DECLAN

*T*he prison was shadowed in the waning sunlight. Gray stones comprised the dull exterior, as well as the two, identical pinnacles on either side of the entrance. A separate building, this one surprisingly modern, stood a little distance away. A wrought iron fence greeted me as I walked up and stood beside a guard tower.

One glance through the small window confirmed that the guard was dead. His intestines were separated from his body.

The humid, Georgian air caused my clothes to stick to my skin. The pungent smell of decaying flesh permeated my nostrils.

An ominous warning was painted in blood over the entrance to the prison.

Beware of Zombies.

Frowning, I considered the dauntingly large structure with calculating eyes. From this distance, I could see figures moving erratically in the fenced-in yard. Ragers. A whole lot of them by the look of it.

I knew, without any doubt, that stepping through this gate would lead to my inevitable death. It was practically mocking me.

Indecision made me pause.

Was I ready to die? Was I ready to leave this world and the girl I loved?

The girl I loved who didn't love me in return?

I thought of the man inside of the prison, the man I was going to kill.

My father.

"Father" was too sentimental of a term to describe that horrid being. We were only related by blood and looks.

The last time I'd seen him, fifteen or so years ago, he had the same long brown hair I used to have. His belly had been large, protruding over the waistband of his jeans, and his eyes had been glacial. This was a man who hadn't seen warmth and certainly didn't know how to distribute it. He was cold, unyielding, and cruel. His fists always had to be pounding into a face, either my own or my mother's, and his lips spewed a constant barrage of poison.

The very last day I saw him, he'd been attacking my mother. Allison had been held tightly in her arms, the little baby blissfully unaware of what a monster her father was. Mother had tried to shield my sister the best she could, but the gesture was futile. One particularly hard hit from my father's drunken rage sent them both sprawling. Mother had obtained only a few bruises, but little Allison's head had ricocheted off of the hardwood floors.

She'd died on impact.

It was that memory, that image of her tiny face, that gave me the courage to move forward. I was going to die. It was something I accepted with an icy detachment. Fear no longer consumed me. Instead, it gave me the courage and strength to do what had to be done. That monster didn't deserve to live, either as a human or as a Rager. He was an insect—an insect I was determined to squish underneath my boot. For once in my life, I wouldn't be the victim around that man. That monster. I would be a fighter. A survivor.

I was going to join Allison and Addie in death.

Maybe, just maybe, that action could redeem me for failing her, failing them both, in the first place.

∼

ADDIE

The boy they led into my room had dark, onyx black hair. A gag was shoved into his mouth, and his hands were tied behind his back. Whimpering, the man's eyes rapidly flickered from face to face.

"What the hell is this?" I directed my question towards Ryder, who was currently leading him into the room.

"*Who* the hell," Doc corrected snidely. I rolled my eyes but didn't humor him with a response. Folding my arms across my chest, I accidentally pushed my ample breasts up. I'd forgotten I was only wearing a lacy black bra that left little to the imagination. Calax subtly—read as totally not subtly—pulled my blanket up to cover me.

"This is Kai," Ronan supplied, waving his arm in Kai's direction.

"Why is Kai tied up with a gag in his mouth?" I asked. "It's not some kind of kinky sex game, is it?" Really, I had to get the important questions out of the way.

Ryder released Kai quickly, a grimace on his handsome face.

"Kitten, you're the only one I want to tie up."

Ignoring him, I said, "Get the gag out of his mouth." My body was heavy, and my eyelids continually threatened to close. The more I talked, the more my words slurred together. "What's happening to me?" This was directed at Doc, who was standing in the corner, arms folded over his impressive chest and a smirk on his face.

"That would be the drugs," he answered.

"Fucking drugs. Why'd you have to drug me? I'm sleepy. Why am I sleepy? Papa Jose would…" I struggled to maintain consciousness. There was something I had to remember. Something important…

"Repeat after me," I slurred. "We don't tie people up unless it's for a sex game. Tying people up is not nice. Drugging people is also not nice."

Vaguely, I realized that the drugs were probably the only reason why I didn't feel any pain. Instead of a blistering, searing pain, my body felt light and buoyant.

"In my defense, he tried to stab me." Ryder said this casually, shrugging his shoulders.

At his words, I saw red. Nobody—and I meant nobody—was allowed to harm my guys.

"Why is he still alive?!" I exclaimed. Kai's eyes widened in terror. Damn right he should be scared. I was a terrifying person when you threatened what was mine. "Bring him here, so I can kill the fucker."

"Ehhh…" Ronan began, while I could've sworn I heard Asher mumble, "So sexy."

"We need to radio Fallon. Let him know you're all right," Calax said gently. He seemed to be trying to distract me from my murderous tendencies. What. An. Asshole.

If you couldn't murder someone, what was the point of life?

And yes, I blamed my thoughts on the drugs.

"Can I take a quick nap first?" I asked, though the words

sounded like a foreign language. Doc, of all people, chuckled. "Suck a dick, Doc."

"Already do," he retorted.

Before I could reply, darkness crept through the corners of my vision. I had one final thought before sleep consumed me. *When did Doc, that fucker, have time to drug me?*

~

I WOKE up to someone whispering my name. Peeling open my crusted eyelids, I stared up at Asher's handsome, boyish face. He held a dark, familiar object in his hand.

A radio.

"I've been talking to Sarge," he said softly. Without breaking eye contact, he pushed a strand of hair behind my ear. "I think it would be good if he heard from you."

The drugs must've been wearing off, as there was a dull throbbing in my stomach that seemed to reverberate throughout my entire body. Still, I smiled and extended a hand for the radio.

After quickly explaining what buttons to push, Asher ducked out of the room. The sky was an inky black, almost velvety in appearance. The candles had long since burned out, leaving only the moon as light.

My heart hammering, I pressed down on the button Asher had indicated.

"Fallon?" I whispered, my voice cracking. I released the button immediately, my breath bated as I waited for him to respond.

There was a crackle of static followed by a disbelieving gasp and then, "Adelaide?"

"I'm here." Tears formed in my eyes, and my throat closed up. Emotions, some of them undefinable, battled within me.

My hand was shaking as I held the radio to my lips. "I'm here. I'm okay."

There was a gasp. Something akin to a sob.

Was Fallon crying?

More tears trailed down my cheeks and landed on my dry lips. I licked them away, tasting salt.

"I'm so… I was so fucking worried."

"I know." And I did know. There was nothing Fallon hated more than being helpless. Than seeing the people he cared about in pain. "But I'm okay. Are you okay?"

"I'm with Tommy and Declan," he replied. "I'll make sure they're okay. And then we'll come home to you."

"Do you promise?" I hated how weak I sounded. How vulnerable. At that moment, I was nothing more than a forlorn child wanting confirmation that she was loved.

"Promise. I'll always come back to you, don't you know that?"

This time, I couldn't keep the sob from escaping. I brought my fist to my mouth to muffle the sound.

"I love you, Fallon." The confession escaped me before I could reel it in. And surprisingly, I didn't want to.

There was silence on the other side.

"I love you too."

"But I—"

"I know. I know. And it's okay. We'll figure it out together. All of us. But I have to go now, okay? I'll see you soon. I love you."

The radio slipped from my fingers, safely landing on the bed. Tears cascaded down my face, but they weren't tears of sadness. No, they were tears of happiness. I couldn't remember the last time I'd felt such contentment.

Not even the pain in my stomach could diminish the elation I felt.

"Addie!"

The bedroom door was thrown open, and Calax stood in the entryway.

"I just finished talking with Fallon." I nodded towards the radio. "I'm going—"

"No time." Before I could protest, Calax scooped me up in his arms. I cried out as pain speared my stomach. "We need to leave. Now."

I bit my lip to keep from crying out, but there was no denying the urgency in Calax's voice. The fear in his eyes. The panic.

"What's going on?" I asked through gritted teeth.

Holding me securely against his chest, Calax turned to face the closed door. From behind it, I could make out growls and shouts, steadily growing louder.

"Ragers. A whole bunch of them."

CHAPTER 24

DECLAN

I couldn't move. My feet were cemented to the ground, my body coiled tightly like a snake preparing to strike. The sun had disappeared behind the gray prison wall, and moonlight took its place. It illuminated the prison yard and the figures with jerky movements and grotesque skin that continued to amble in the gated confines.

My hands trembled.

What it came down to was whether or not I was ready to die. The longer I stood there, debating my options, the more gray the world became. My courage ebbed simultaneously with the sun lowering. What had I been thinking?

I took a tentative step forward.

"Why are you in a bad mood?" I signed to Addie as she entered the kitchen. Sweat coated her skin in a glossy sheen, and a few stray curls escaped her ponytail. Even with the scar on her face from that bitch, Liz, she was still the most beautiful woman I'd ever

feasted my eyes upon. It was impossible for me to look away, as if she had her own magnetic orb. I was lost in her gaze.

"Fallon is an asshole," *she replied, her hands moving rapidly to hint at her own agitation. I snorted but didn't contradict. Sarge was an asshole. No one could deny that.*

"Why is he an asshole?" *My lips curved upward instinctively. She was adorable all pissed off, though I doubted she would agree with such a sentiment. Like a puppy.*

"He's making me exercise." *Her face twisted in horror.* "I don't exercise. Ever." *Her hands dropped as she absentmindedly began to ramble about the dangers of working out. I could've sworn her lips said,* "It makes my boobs sag."

But I could've been mistaken.

She paused suddenly, her lips clamping into a tight line. Her eyes flickered to the doorway that led to the backyard, and something akin to fear flashed in her gaze. Before I could inquire, she had thrown herself underneath the table and sidled to sit between my legs.

I froze, peering down at her with wide eyes. With the way she was positioned...

I shifted uncomfortably, praying she didn't see how hard I'd become. Fortunately, she remained blissfully oblivious to my predicament as she put a single finger to her red lips.

Raising my eyebrow in confusion—really, I should've just expected as much from that crazy female—I noticed a figure move in my peripheral vision.

Sarge entered the kitchen, eyes narrowing.

"Have you seen Adelaide?" *he asked.* "She ran out in the middle of training. Claimed that her boobs had come undone, whatever that meant."

I didn't even have to look to know that Addie would've been shaking her head rapidly beneath the table.

"No," *I signed, nodding towards the old newspaper in front of me.* "I've been reading."

Sarge glared, as if doubting my sincerity, before he stomped away.

I waited until he was out of sight before pulling up the table cloth and peering once more at Addie. Her hand was over her mouth as she restrained a giggle. Her eyes were alit with mirth.

Briefly, she rested her chin on my knee.

"My hero," she said, moving her lips slowly enough for me to read. At this point, I was pretty sure I had those things memorized. When I dreamt, it was about those damn plush lips. What I wouldn't have given to taste them...

Keeping my face impassive, I nodded.

"Always."

Always.

I was such a horrible liar.

There was a name for someone like me. Narcissist. Selfish.

I'd broken my promise. I'd left her after I'd promised to always be by her side. Maybe I hadn't said it in so many words, but I'd meant it. She was mine. After years of forced separation, I would never leave her side again.

But...

Groaning, I pulled at my dark hair. The physical pain somehow diminished my mental one. More. I needed more.

I took another step towards the large structure, knowing that I was both literally and figuratively walking to my death.

A hand clamped down on my shoulder, making me stagger back. Stunned, I turned to meet Sarge's burning eyes.

The car headlights switched on, illuminating his face.

"I knew I would find you here," he signed. I watched his hands move in rapt fascination.

"How?"

Nobody knew about this place. Nobody. I'd made sure that this—he—had remained a secret. It was my burden to shoulder alone. I couldn't discern if it was embarrassment or shame. After all, what type of person wanted to claim relation to an abusive, murderous asshole? Would they think we were one and the same, cut from the same tree or however that saying went?

"Did you believe I wouldn't do my research on the team?" was his simple answer.

I scoffed.

Of course he would. He was Sarge.

Two figures in the car captured my attention. Tommy I recognized straight away, but he was talking animatedly to an unfamiliar boy wearing thick, red headphones around his neck.

Nikolai.

He had the same bone structure and hair color as Addie.

I turned back towards Sarge.

"You found him? He's all right?"

His face softened as he nodded.

"He is. And I heard from Addie."

At those words, my body tensed. I scarcely believed it. Addie was dying. I'd seen the life drain from her eyes, had held her cold, icy hand in my own. Was he saying…?

"She's okay. Addie is okay." He took a step closer. "And she wants us to come home."

Addie was okay.

A weight from my chest was lifted at those words. It was as if I could finally breathe again, finally live.

Helplessly, I glanced once more at the prison. Sarge tapped my shoulder, redirecting my attention back to him. His eyes were very near pleading, something I was unfamiliar seeing on the apathetic team leader.

"She needs you. The team needs you. I know what you're thinking. I know that you want to get revenge on your father, but we both know that walking up there is a death sentence. Addie is waiting, and she loves you. Don't break her heart like this."

Tears blurred my vision.

Loved? She loved me?

Surely, Sarge was mistaken. She loved Calax and maybe even Ryder. Not me.

Never me.

It was a fantasy I used to have, though I never believed we would be the traditional couple. I had too many demons, too many jagged edges. She, on the other hand, was a bright fucking light. But I would've been the first to admit that if she was the sun, I was her shadow, following her to the end of the world like a diligent pup. Sometimes, when the darkness was too much for people to handle, they craved the light. It was a selfish mentality but undeniably true. I needed her because she was the light to my tarnished darkness.

I'd been horrible to her when we reconnected. It became clear that we behaved the worst to the people we loved because we knew they would never leave us. But god, she had come so close. More than once. With her, it felt like I could fall and always have someone at the bottom catching me.

"When have I ever lied to you?" Sarge snapped, easily reading the indecision and disbelief on my face.

Before I realized what was happening, I collapsed against him, sobbing. It wasn't a manly cry by any means. Oh no. It was a collection of snot and tears and gasps. Sarge remained rigid, unsure how to comfort me, before awkwardly patting my back.

I cried for Addie and all she'd endured.

I cried for my mom, choosing to live a life on the streets to feed her addiction. She'd chosen drugs over her own son. Over me.

I cried for my baby sister, whose life had been snuffed out too early.

And I cried for myself. The realization came crashing down on me, the onslaught bordering the precarious line between pain and relief.

I couldn't do it. I couldn't sacrifice my life for a twisted version of vengeance.

I'm so sorry, Allison.

Everything became simple. Black and white instead of a thousand shades of grey.

I was choosing Addie, as I'd done countless times before. And maybe, just maybe, she'd chosen me back.

∾

ADDIE

Calax's arms were iron vises around me as he set the radio into my lap. I gripped it tightly in my hand. Distantly, I was aware of a screeching coming from outside the house. The sound was getting louder and louder with each passing second.

"They're here!" Ryder stood in the doorway, eyes wild and face ashen.

"What's going on?" I asked, anxiously glancing from face to face.

"Some asshole is driving a police car with the sirens blaring," Ryder said through clenched teeth. "It led the Ragers right to us."

Fear paralyzed me, sparking down my spine and to the toes of my feet.

"Who would do such a thing?" Either someone was an idiot or...this was intentional. But who? Questions assaulted me, but I knew now was not the time to get answers.

"Ronan and Asher are collecting more supplies from the hospital," Ryder informed us as we moved down the long hallway and to the staircase. "We'll meet them there. Tamson is starting the car. Doc and Kai are with him."

"Weapons?" Calax asked, hurrying his pace. The siren was just outside our house now, the sound very near deafening.

"None with me," Ryder replied briskly. Before anyone could say anything else, there was the sound of a window shattering. Fine particles of glass flung through the air, a few keen shards nicking my skin.

A Rager crawled through the window.

Its body held evidence of the recent surge of acid rain. Peeling skin, darkening to a sickly red color. Hair leaving its head in clumps. Brittle bone appearing at intermittent intervals throughout its body. It...or was it a he? His genitals were on full display, somehow demoting him from a monster to a human.

Ryder lunged, slamming into the Rager's deformed body and taking them both to the ground. His fingers dug into the creature's neck, loose skin breaking until the brittle, offset white bone was revealed. I turned my face into Calax's chest, resisting the urge to vomit, as the putrid stench of blood bombarded my senses.

The creature writhed and bucked beneath Ryder, but he held firm, never once removing his hands from the Rager's neck.

With a sudden burst of strength, the Rager shoved Ryder off of him. Blood and skin dribbled down his face as he leaned over my lover.

"No!" I screamed, voice a mere rasp. At the noise, the creature's feral gaze whipped in my direction. There was nothing remotely human in his red, pinprick eyes. He was a shell of a man. The monster had completely overtaken him. I was wrong in my initial assessment. Not a he. An it.

Ryder used its distraction to slide out from underneath, crawling towards the door. There was an ugly gash in his chest that hadn't been there before, but otherwise, he looked relatively unharmed.

"Shit," Calax murmured, arms tightening around me. He took a step backwards, eyes locked on the creature...

Until a rough hand grabbed at us from behind. Calax let out a curse, shielding my body more firmly with his own. The new Rager clambered through the broken window, clawed hand snaring Calax's shirt. Another one appeared over her shoulder, this one just as grotesque as all the others. More and more were invading the house, circling us like we were prey and they were the hunters. I supposed it wasn't an inaccurate analogy.

There were too many of them.

Too few of us.

I could hear the car start from nearby, and I prayed that Tamson had made it to safety. It was a futile prayer, but a prayer nonetheless.

"We need to go!" Ryder shouted. He stood behind the throng of Ragers, fists raised as he prepared to fight.

But there were just too many. Swarming us. Surrounding us. Gnawing at us. Calax let out a scream as a Rager bit down on his arm, blood spewing from his mouth. I gagged at the pungent copper scent.

I could see the exact moment that he came to the same conclusion I had. His brow had been furrowed, but just then, it smoothed over. His eyes turned warm as they traced my face.

"I love you so much, baby girl," he whispered, brushing his lips against my forehead. I trembled in his arms, the realization that we were going to die drowning me. I wanted to check out, to mentally leave this horrible place, but I couldn't leave Calax alone. At the end, we only had each other.

The rest of the world fell away—the Ragers' inarticulate cries, Ryder's scream of agony, the car engine only a wall away. Nothing mattered but the arms of my first love.

We'd survived so much together. Our lives were forever interwoven. He held a piece of my heart in his large, calloused hands, and I held a piece of his. They may have been broken individually, but together, they became whole.

"I love you too," I whispered, knowing that those would be the last words I ever said. I could only hope that the others would forgive me, forgive us, when all was said and done. Hopelessness settled over me, over us, like a death shroud. My heart was beating so rapidly, it sounded like a snare drum in my ears.

Steely determination crossed Calax's face, and his arms tightened around me. Before I realized what was happening, we were moving.

The Ragers clawed at us, their fingers gnarled, keen knives. Calax bellowed in agony, but still he continued to trudge forward. Before I could blink, before I could beg, I was flying through the air. That was the only word I could think to describe it.

My body soared, slamming into Ryder's a few feet away. Agony speared my stomach as my stitches came undone, and blood seeped through my new shirt.

And...

"Calax!" I screamed, scrambling to my feet. Ryder immediately picked me up bridal style, turning towards the doorway.

But I still saw.

I saw the Ragers converging on a fallen figure, tearing through his flesh. I saw the tip of his brown boot, now soaked with blood. I heard his anguished screams as the monsters ate away at his flesh.

"Calax!" I screamed hysterically. Ignoring the pain, I

bucked against Ryder's hold. Pounded on his chest. Sobbed. Begged. "Calax! We have to get Calax! We have to go back!"

His face was pained, tears forming in his golden-brown eyes. He finally met my gaze, even as he carried me farther and farther away.

"There's nothing we can do," he whispered.

I refused to believe that. Calax needed me, needed us. He had to be okay. He just had to. The alternative was too horrible to even consider.

I was screaming, agony piercing my chest as my heart broke into thousands of pieces. I struggled futilely against Ryder's hold, Calax's screams still haunting me.

No. No. No.

"Calax!" I screamed into the night sky. "Calax!"

Darkness crept along the edges of my vision. Blood soaked through my hands that were now resting on my stomach. I didn't care about the pain. When more Ragers ran towards the house, bypassing both Ryder and me, I realized that Calax wasn't coming out.

"CALAX!"

Darkness consumed me.

CHAPTER 25

ADDIE

*T*here was a lake I used to visit.

Perhaps 'lake' was too strong of a term for the diminutive pool of water. Big enough to fit the occasional speedboat. Small enough where you were easily able to see the opposite shoreline. It glistened in the sunlight, tiny crystal beads, and gently crested against the grassy shoreline. The air had been thinner there. Fresher. With the serene water rippling in tandem with each passing boat, I'd felt nothing but tranquility standing on the shore. Grass tickled my toes, and my hair carried in the breeze.

Couples often visited this particular shoreline. Dancing in the firelight. Kissing. Laughing.

Free.

Just like the water.

It was one of my happy places, that lake, with the throng of trees and rows of immaculate mansions stretching the shoreline. The beach had barely any sand. Instead, grass and dirt greeted my bare feet. It was this image, this calm pool of water, that helped me fabricate my mental garden, the garden I'd created inside of my mind in order to survive.

My mental garden was actually a combination of many locations. The old house I'd visited with Ducky. The pond behind Calax's apartment building. The schoolyard.

I went there then as Ryder held me tightly in his arms, shielding my body with his own. I barely processed when he laid me down on the backseat of the car, screaming directions up to Tamson. I heard Doc's voice, and then felt hands press down on my bleeding stomach. I felt that all before I drifted away.

In my garden, there was a simple stone bench beneath a white painted archway. Flowers and vines climbed up the sides, intricate patterns that combined perennials with blood red tulips and purple violets. The odd combination was almost ethereal in beauty.

Peace.

I felt peace in my garden.

But all good things couldn't last.

As I watched the frosted waves, I became aware of a figure moving to sit beside me on the stone bench. His body emitted heat, and I yearned to sink into his embrace. I hadn't even realized I was cold until I came face to face with a human furnace.

"What are you doing here?" Calax asked softly. I absently brushed my fingers over a silky rose petal. It was beginning to wilt and decay. Everything had an expiration date.

Everything died.

"It's better in here than out there," I responded. The real world. My own personal hell.

"So you're just retreating?" he asked in disbelief.

"Are you dead?" I countered.

His face turned contemplative. His hand snaked up to rub at his scruffy jaw.

"You keep me alive," he said after an agonizingly long moment of silence. I snorted.

No, I had most definitely *not* kept him alive.

"I like this place," I said, changing the subject. "You're here with me."

"Always."

He leaned forward, resting his elbows on his jean-clad legs. I was once again struck by how handsome he was. With his shock of dark hair framing an arresting, chiseled face, he was the epitome of perfection.

And he was mine.

"Why did you sacrifice yourself for me?" I whispered, the words catching in my throat. I tried to hold back the sob that threatened to escape. "Why?"

That was the question for all things in life—why?

Why did Calax have to die?

Why did I have to live?

Why? Why? Why?

"I don't want to live without you." These words were a broken plea. Salty tears dripped down my cheeks. Pain. Pain everywhere. All I'd ever known was pain. I'd hoped I could leave my love behind like breadcrumbs for him to follow home. But what if love wasn't enough? Love couldn't conquer death, no matter how much we wished otherwise. We could weave stories of friendships and families, of love and pain, but there was always something that trumped it. The ominous death hung over us like a bloated storm cloud threatening to expel its contents.

"I know, baby girl. I know. But you're going to have to wake up now. The others need you."

"No!" I answered instantly, clutching at his large bicep. I

wanted to mold my body into his. I wanted us to become one. "I'm not leaving you."

"Don't let my sacrifice be in vain. I love you too much for that. Wake up."

I was sobbing now, unashamed by my show of emotion. How did he expect me to go on? To pretend that everything was okay, and I wasn't falling apart at the seams? This was how you could die while still breathing. A broken heart hurt worse than thousands of gunshots to the stomach.

Calax cupped my face tenderly and pressed his lips against mine. It was a slow kiss, different from any other I'd ever experienced before. I trembled once in his arms.

"I love you," I whispered.

"Wake up for me."

Wake up.

Wake up.

And I woke up.

EPILOGUE

CALAX

*V*oices.

Some indistinct murmurs. Some louder.

None of them were hers.

"The girl here?" This voice sounded just over my head.

Was I dying? Was this death?

"That's a negative. Look at this fuck. Is he still alive?" Somebody touched my neck.

"Barely. Think we should have Michaels check him over?"

"If he knows where the girl is…"

The voices trailed off, and I mercifully drifted back to sleep.

~

I AWOKE to someone touching me. Poking me.

Pain. Agonizing pain.

A scream escaped my lips before I could smother it.

"Shut him up, will ya?"

My eyes were blurry, barely able to focus, but they did latch onto a figure leaning over me. White lab coat. Gray hair. A doctor.

And behind him?

Two masked figures.

One a lion. One a plain white mask with red eyes.

I struggled to hold onto consciousness, but it pulled me under. Frankly, it was better than the pain.

So much pain.

Pain.

Darkness.

ACKNOWLEDGMENTS

Thank you to my family for sticking with me and supporting me. You guys are incredible, and I don't know where I would be without your help and guidance.

Thank you to my readers who took a chance on me when I had no idea what I was doing. Your support and love for this series constantly blows me away. I love you all.

And finally, thank *you*. Yes, you! The person currently reading this. I love you to the moon and back. Thank you for loving Addie and her men as much as I do.

ABOUT THE AUTHOR

Katie May is a reverse harem author, a KDP All-Star winner, and an USA Today Bestselling Author. She lives in West Michigan with her family and cat. When not writing, she could be found reading a good book, listening to broadway musicals, or playing games. Join Katie's Gang to stay updated on all her releases! And did you know she has a TikTok? Yeah, me either. Follow her here! But be warned...she's an awkward noodle.

ALSO BY KATIE MAY

Together We Fall (Apocalyptic Reverse Harem, COMPLETED)

1. The Darkness We Crave

2. The Light We Seek

3. The Storm We Face

4. The Monsters We Hunt

Beyond the Shadows (Horror Reverse Harem, COMPLETED)

1. Gangs and Ghosts

2. Guns and Graveyards

3. Gallows and Ghouls

The Damning (Fantasy Paranormal Reverse Harem)

1. Greed

2. Envy

3. Gluttony

Prodigium Academy (Horror Comedy Academy Reverse Harem)

1. Monsters

2. Roaring

Tory's School for the Trouble (Bully Horror Academy Reverse Harem)

1. Between

2. Beyond (Coming Soon)

Supernaturalette (Interactive Reverse Harem)

1. Introductions

2. First Dates

3. Group Outing

4. Game Night

5. Exes

Kingdom of Wolves (Shifter Reverse Harem Duet)

1. Torn to Bits

2. Ripped to Shreds

CO-WRITES

Afterworld Academy with Loxley Savage (Academy Fantasy Reverse Harem)

1. Dearly Departed

2. Darkness Deceives

3. Defying Destiny

Darkest Flames with Ann Denton (Paranormal Reverse Harem)

1. Demon Kissed

1.5. Demon Stalked

2. Demon Loved

3. Demon Sworn

STAND-ALONES

Toxicity (Contemporary Reverse Harem)

Blindly Indicted (Prison Reverse Harem)

Not All Heroes Wear Capes (Just Dresses) (Short Comedic Reverse Harem)

Charming Devils (Bully/Revenge Reverse Harem)

Goddess of Pain (Fantasy Reverse Harem)

Demon's Joy (Holiday Reverse Harem)

Made in the USA
Columbia, SC
18 December 2021

51962348R00136